THE
PARKER TWINS
S E R I E S

Mystery at Death Canyon

THE PARKER TWINS SERIES

4

THE PARKER TWINS SERIES

Mystery at Death Canyon

JEANETTE WINDLE

Kregel Publications

Mystery at Death Canyon

© 1996, 2002 by Jeanette Windle

Published by Kregel Publications, a division of Kregel, Inc., P.O. Box 2607, Grand Rapids, MI 49501. For more information about Kregel Publications, visit our Web site: www.kregel.com.

Cover illustration: Patrick Kelley
Cover design: John M. Lucas

ISBN 0-8254-4148-x

Printed in the United States of America

1 2 3 4 5 / 06 05 04 03 02

POISON!

The boy lying huddled against the rock face halfway down the cliff drew in a long, shuddering breath. The night smelled clean and fresh, giving no hint of the death it carried. A full moon shed a gentle light across the boulder-strewn canyon floor below him. Far above, on the flat surface of the plateau, the distant beat of drums lulled the small prairie creatures into a dreamless sleep.

The night's quiet beauty brought no comfort to Justin. He had only to glance over the edge of the narrow ledge to see the bleached bones and rotting shapes that were animals trapped, as he had been, by this innocent-looking canyon. Would he be its next victim?

He nodded drowsily, yawning against the tape that gagged his mouth. Already, he could feel the canyon's slow poison seeping into his body, weighing down his head. With fresh panic, he twisted and pulled on the bonds that held him. It was useless! His captors knew their business too well.

Hot rage swept away his fear as he caught sight of the two dark figures silhouetted on the canyon rim. Were all the hopes— all the dreams—for the people of these windswept prairies to be shattered because of a few men's greed? It just wasn't fair!

A breeze stirred in the canyon, its touch cool on Justin's face. He lay still, his chest heaving. Anger and panic drained slowly away as his gaze traveled upward from the canyon rim to the hot sparks of fire that were constellations blazing against the black velvet of the summer sky. *Are you still up there, God? Do you know what is going on down here?*

He yawned again, blinking sleepily. He hardly noticed when the light of the moon dimmed in contrast to the ghostly horseman who filled the night sky above the canyon. Strange colored lights flickered along the warrior's uplifted spear and flashed from the soundless hooves of his spotted pony. Dreamily, Justin watched the stars glint slowly through the warrior's long black hair.

As the ghost of Death Canyon galloped swiftly down the canyon, vanishing into the night, Justin no longer fought the weight that pressed down on his eyelids. *"Jenny, don't let them get away with this!"* he mumbled. Then deadly slumber swept him away.

Chapter One

LOST

Justin's nostrils twitched in his sleep. Though he knew vaguely that he was dreaming, the leaping flames of the campfire beside which he squatted were hot and acrid and very real. He was on the Indian reservation, that much he recognized. But somehow he had shifted though a time warp because the men hunkered around the campfire with him were wearing U.S. Army Cavalry uniforms. And those Indians riding up over the bluff were carrying real bows and lances.

Justin dodged a spear throw, the sudden move rubbing his sunburned shoulders against the back of the car seat. The discomfort pulled him out of his dream so that the campfire faded and he could hear a distant voice that belonged to his twin. Strangely, the sharp burning smell of the campfire still lingered. "Come on, Dad, tell me about this place we're visiting!" Jenny was demanding. "And this John McCloud. Who is he? Why haven't you ever told us about him before? It just sounds so exciting—a real Indian reservation! And where is the place, anyway? You said we were almost there, but all I've seen for hours is prairie grass and sage brush."

"I've already told you, Jenny." The new voice was Dad's, deep and teasing. "You'll get your answers when we get to the reservation. Besides, I thought you and Justin had all the excitement you could want for one summer."

That was true! Dad, a computer analyst consultant who worked for Boeing in Seattle, Washington, had been too busy finishing a contract for one of the airplane company's new planes to take a family vacation earlier in the summer. Instead, Ron and Helen Parker had allowed their thirteen-year-old twins to accompany Uncle Pete, an executive with Triton Oil, on a business/vacation trip to South America. There Justin and Jenny had found themselves tangling with smugglers, drug dealers, and guerrillas in one hair-raising adventure after another.

Still, that had been a month ago, and the weeks in between had been quiet and boring. Then Dad had finished his project earlier than expected, making it possible to accept this John McCloud's invitation to an Indian reservation in eastern)Nontana. Even in the twenty-first century, an Indian reservation promised adventure. Horses! Rodeos! A real Indian tribe!

Justin was wide awake now. But . . . why was he still smelling that campfire? He opened his eyes, then sat up abruptly. "Dad, stop the car! We're on fire!"

Dad broke off his teasing in mid-sentence, one eyebrow raised as he glanced into the rearview mirror. Wordlessly, Justin pointed out the windshield where dark smoke poured from the hood.

"Oh, no!" Dad slammed on the brakes. Switching off the ignition, he leaned over to shake Mom awake. "Get out of the car!"

Mom was already sitting up, drowsy eyes blinking with alarm. Unsnapping his seatbelt, Dad jumped down from the driver's seat and raced around to the passenger side. By the time Justin and Jenny had unfastened their own seatbelts and scrambled out, he had yanked open the passenger door and was helping Mom from the front seat.

"Keep moving!" Dad directed them down over the embankment of the highway, herding them a full fifty yards from the road before he waved them to a stop. The four Parkers turned to look back at the dark green Trooper SUV, deserted up on the highway. Smoke still seeped from under the hood, but nothing else seemed to be happening.

Pulling out a handkerchief, Dad blew his nose. "I'm sorry, guys. I should have smelled that smoke, but this hay fever of mine!"

Mom slipped a hand into Dad's arm. "What happened, Ron?"

"I'm not sure. I knew the engine was getting warm, but I hoped to coax it the last few miles to Rocky Creek. I didn't even notice when it started smoking!"

Dad threw a long arm around Justin's shoulders. "If it hadn't been for Justin here, we might have burned to a crisp!"

Justin's chest swelled. "It wasn't really *all* that much!" Looking down, he kicked at the dust with the toe of his tennis shoe. "I just . . ."

"Rocky Creek!" interrupted Jenny. Justin frowned. Couldn't his sister see she was interrupting his big moment? But Jenny ignored his annoyed glare and rushed on. "You mean, we're already on the reservation?"

"On the boundary, anyway." Dad pointed to a large, brown sign up on the highway: Entering Tribal Lands—Big Sky Indian Reservation.

Justin forgot his irritation. "Hey cool! So when do we get to see the Indians? Uh, Native Americans, I mean."

"Either term will do here in Montana," Dad said. "As you can see by that sign. As for meeting Indians—or Native Americans—you'll get your share soon enough."

"Yeah, so where are they?" Jenny demanded skeptically, turning around in a slow circle. "Or anyone? This doesn't look any different than what we've seen all day."

Justin turned around and looked. She was right! The dry, dusty grasslands that rolled in every direction seemed no different than the prairies they'd driven through since early morning. Only one thing broke the line of the horizon—a flat-topped rock formation that looked like an enormous table for giants. Nowhere did he see any sign of human habitation.

"Yeah, if this is a reservation, where are the people?" he echoed. "This looks like we're out in the middle of the wilderness."

"I can see you two don't understand the size of an Indian reservation. The Big Sky Indian Reservation is small as reservations go, but it's more than 150,000 acres." Dad waved toward the massive rock formation. "But we can't be too far from civilization. John McCloud told me there was a mesa, a tableland, just a few miles out of Rocky Creek."

"John McCloud?" Jenny demanded. "There you go again. Just who is this guy?"

But Dad didn't hear her; he was already heading back toward the car.

"Okay, guys, it doesn't look like it's going to blow. Let's see what we can do to get this heap back on the road." He popped open the hood, and his head and shoulders disappeared in a cloud of steam and black smoke. "I don't see any fire!" He shook his head sadly. "I guess I should have traded this wreck in before the trip. I'd hoped it would make one more trip." He gave the hot metal of the hood a pat. "Well, that's it for you, old girl! You're going to the dump just as soon as we get back. Justin, the tool chest!"

Justin grinned as he walked around to the rear of the car to pull out the tool chest. The Trooper SUV was one of the original models, more than ten years old, and breakdowns were a familiar part of family vacations. But Dad loved the old wreck—partly because it was already so banged up it didn't mind the dings and dents of fishing trips and other family expeditions. Maybe this time Dad would give in to Mom's pleading and trade it in. Maybe!

Dad took the tool chest and dug around inside. "It looks like the gas line sprung a leak. A small one, thank God! But I'm afraid the heater hose is pretty well shot!"

Justin edged closer and peered over his father's back. It wasn't the first time he'd helped with this engine, and he could easily piece together what had gone wrong. A tiny leak in the gas line sprayed gasoline across the hot engine. Luckily the engine hadn't caught fire, but the gas melted the heater hose into a black, gooey mess. And now the radiator was completely dry.

Dad wiped his hands on a rag. "We could probably mend that gas line to last ten miles. But we aren't going anywhere without water!"

Justin glanced across the landscape. There *must* be water somewhere around here. But the parched prairie grass was only broken by dry clumps of sagebrush as far as he could see. There was no hint of green to signal a pond or stream.

Highway traffic had been light since the Parkers left the

Rockies behind that morning. But after turning onto this secondary road, they had passed only an occasional camper and a few sturdy pickups, usually with a dog or two bracing themselves against the wind in the back. Now there wasn't a single car in sight. Compared to the busy Seattle freeways, Justin found this immense, empty terrain a little eerie.

"You guys might as well make yourselves comfortable. I'm afraid we're stuck until someone comes along!" Dad strode around to the back of the car. "Now if I can just find something to plug that heater hose."

No stranger to unexpected delays, Mom climbed calmly back into the front seat. A freelance writer, she was most likely dreaming up a new book idea or article. But Justin had no intentions of joining her. He turned to Dad, but Jenny took the words out of his mouth. "Oh, Dad, we're so tired of sitting! Can't we go for a walk or something?"

Dad rummaged in the spare tire compartment, then pulled out a rusty bolt and a piece of wire. He nodded. "Okay! But not too far." As the twins broke into a run, Dad called, "Half an hour—someone will be along by then!"

Sliding down the embankment, Justin and Jenny walked alongside the highway. A cloudless sky stretched overhead, but a late-afternoon breeze laid cooling fingers against Justin's sunburn. He wished he'd taken Jenny's advice yesterday at the motel pool. He looked enviously at his twin as she stopped to watch a small herd of horses. All she got from their hours of splashing was more golden tan—a nice contrast to her dark hair. It just wasn't fair! He ran his fingers through his short-cropped red hair. Who would have ever guessed they were really twins?

Several colts frisked among the calmly grazing mothers, nipping each other in an equine game of tag. One mischievous colt decided to include his mother in the game. The mare snorted. Her expression was so much like a human mother as she gave her colt a stern nip that Jenny giggled. "Oh, Justin, aren't they cute!"

"I guess," he shrugged. "Come *on,* Jenny! I want to explore!"

Jenny wrinkled her nose at her brother, but she stretched her long legs in a sprint that soon left him behind. When he finally caught her, she was standing at the edge of a narrow gorge. He skidded to a stop beside her.

It looked like a small stream sometimes ran through this gorge. Justin climbed up to the highway to peer under the bridge. But the creek bed was hard and cracked. He turned to look upstream. The gorge ran in a direct line toward the massive tableland that marked the boundary of the Big Sky Indian Reservation. His hazel eyes suddenly brightened.

"Hey, let's head upstream! Maybe we can find some water!"

He scrambled down, but Jenny hesitated. "Dad said half an hour."

"We're fine. Besides, he'll be glad if we find some water!"

"Well, okay. As long as we're not late!"

She slid down to join him, and they set off in the direction of the mesa. Their path was choked by various-sized boulders, carried downstream by the spring floods. They jumped from one boulder to the next, making their way steadily upstream. But the gorge narrowed, and the footing grew dangerous. When the creek bed made an abrupt turn to the right, they abandoned the gorge and climbed up the bank to the grasslands above.

"Well, *I* sure didn't see any water!" Jenny flopped down on the ground.

Justin ignored her. Climbing to the top of a small rise, he looked back down the gorge. They had come a long way, but he could still make out the highway and a tiny figure that was his father bent over the front of the SUV. He turned around. The late-afternoon sun had traveled far to the west, and the soaring wall of the mesa now cast a long shadow across the prairie. It looked tantalizingly close. He glanced down at his sister, now stretched out on the grass.

"Hey, Jenny, don't quit now! We can still make it to the mesa if we cut straight across!"

"What for?" Jenny folded her arms stubbornly under her head. "I'm tired—and it's getting late!"

Justin sighed. How could he explain to her that the challenge of *getting* somewhere was all the reason needed. "Maybe there's water over there! Anyway, *I'm* going to check it out. You can stay here if you want."

Justin started down the rise. Jenny let out an exasperated breath, but scrambled to her feet. Justin turned. "So, you decided to come along."

"That's because I know when you start checking things out, we're headed for trouble. You need me to keep an eye on you." She set off at a trot across the prairie. "Well, come on, Justin! If we're going to do it, let's do it!"

He quickly caught her, but they hadn't gone far before he realized that the mesa was farther away than he thought, and the prairie wasn't as flat as it looked. Instead, it rose and fell in gentle swells, broken frequently by crevices or grass-filled hollows. The prickly sagebrush and sharp-edged prairie grass scratched at their bare legs. They climbed down into another shallow gully to pick their way toward the long shadow of the mesa.

The gully came to an abrupt end, and Jenny glanced at her watch. "Justin, look at the time! We've got to go back!"

He wanted to reach the overhanging shadow of the mesa, but nodded reluctantly. "We'll be late if we go down the gully. Let's cut across the top."

He scrambled to the top of the sloping dirt bank. The mesa loomed only a short distance ahead now, but where was their car? He scanned the horizon for the highway, but it too had disappeared!

Jenny looked around with dismay, "Are we lost?"

"Of course we're not lost!" Justin snapped. "The highway's right over there; we'll just walk straight away from the mesa. But we'd better hurry or we'll be late!"

"You're telling me!" she muttered. She broke into a run, and Justin sprinted after her. Jenny was the faster, but Justin had more endurance, and it was Jenny who finally threw herself on the ground, breathless and laughing.

Justin dropped down beside her. Just ahead, the ground sloped into a wide, grassy hollow. Hundreds of knee-high mounds dotted the hollow like earthen beehives. Justin ran his hand through his hair. They hadn't passed this place before! Where was the highway? They should have seen it by now!

"Hey, it's one of those prairie dog towns! Aren't they adorable?"

Justin hardly glanced at the squirrel-like animals that watched from atop their homes. He searched the area for any landmark that might lead them back to the car. His heart sank when he realized he no longer knew where they were. To make matters worse, yesterday's sunburn and today's trek had turned his skin into a raging fire. What a way to start his vacation!

A prairie dog popped its head out of a mound just a few feet away and gave an inquisitive chirp. Jenny leaned against his shoulder and whispered, "Look. That one wants to make friends."

"Hey! Cool it, will you!"

She pulled away, her golden-brown eyes flashing at his angry remark. She opened her mouth for a smart retort then noticed his expression of real pain. "Oh, Justin, you look awful! You're sure going to be sore tonight!"

"Tell me about it," he grumbled. "I'm sorry Jenny. It's just . . ."

"That's okay. I'm sorry I hurt your sunburn." She tried to look sympathetic, but couldn't suppress a giggle. "You know, with skin the same color as your hair, you look just like a giant strawberry!" She eyed the dried sun screen that still streaked his arms. "Strawberry and cream, that is!"

He forced a smile at her teasing, but she knew him too well. "We really *are* lost, aren't we?" she asked gently.

He hunched his shoulders in a helpless shrug. "It all looks the same!"

Jenny stood up and put her hands on her hips. "I just *knew* something like this would happen! So, now what?"

Justin scanned the horizon. It seemed like the highway should be nearby, but it was nowhere to be seen. They were definitely lost.

A movement several hundred yards away caught Justin's eye, and he jumped to his feet. Yes, there it was! Riding out from the shadow of the mesa came a broad figure on a gray horse. A black hat hid the face, but Justin could make out a knapsack over one shoulder and what looked like a shovel or pick balanced across the saddle.

Cupping his hands to his mouth, he shouted, "Hey, you over there! Can you please help us? We're lost! We need help!"

Turning around, Jenny saw the rider and added her own shouts to Justin's, waving frantically and jumping up and down. Unless the rider was deaf and blind, he had to hear and see them, but he just swung his horse around and disappeared to the other side of the mesa.

"Great!" Justin's sunburned shoulders slumped. "Now what?"

But Jenny didn't answer. She grabbed his arm and whispered, "Justin, tell me. Am I dreaming?"

"Ouch!" He turned impatiently, peeling her fingers off his sunburned arm. "Of course you're not dreaming!" Then his own eyes widened as he followed her gaze to a grassy rise that had been deserted just moments before. There on a horse was a figure right out of a history book! Black braids framed a smooth bronzed face. From the beaded band on his forehead, a cascade of white feathers swept down to the shoulders of a knee-length leather tunic. Cream-colored leggings and a pair of beaded moccasins completed the traditional dress of an Indian chieftain. Justin rubbed his eyes in disbelief, but the tall figure remained.

Arms folded across a broad chest, the Indian chieftain watched them, his dark eyes unblinking. Afternoon heat waves shimmered across the grass, slightly blurring the strange image.

"You . . . you don't think it's a ghost, do you?" Jenny mouthed to Justin.

"Of course not! There's no such thing as ghosts!" Justin whispered back. "Well, if he's real, maybe he can help us find our way."

Justin warily eyed the Indian's expressionless dark features. "He might not understand us." He took a startled step backward as the Indian chieftain suddenly dismounted the horse, unfolded his arms, and moved forward.

"Is there something I can do for you kids?" he asked in perfect English.

Justin's mouth dropped open. Before he could shut it, Jenny blurted out, "We're lost! Could you please help us find our parents?"

The fringe on his leather-clad arm swayed as he pointed to a small hill. "Cross that rise, and it's about a five minute walk to your car. Your father just filled the radiator, so I'd get a move on, Justin and Jenny!"

They both turned to follow the direction of his pointing finger. "Wow!" Justin exclaimed. "I didn't think there still *were* any real Indian chiefs! Wait until we tell Dad!" Suddenly the Indian's last words registered. Justin whirled around. "Wait a minute! How did you know our names?"

His voice trailed off. The grassy rise was empty. One hand over his eyes, Justin searched the horizon. The knee-high grasses swayed slightly under a faint breeze, the horse remained, but there was no sign of another human being anywhere on the vast prairie.

Chapter Two

JOHN MCCLOUD

Justin and Jenny scrambled up the rise the strange Indian had pointed out. Sure enough, only a few hundred yards away, they could make out the figure of their father bent over the engine.

They were hot and out of breath by the time they reached the highway. Dad slammed down the hood as they approached. Reaching the SUV, Justin burst out, "I'm really sorry we're so late, Dad! We got a little lost!"

"Yeah, and we were rescued by a real Indian chief! At least . . . I think he was real." Jenny looked doubtfully at Justin. "We didn't imagine it, did we? Like one of those mirages people see in the desert?"

"No, he knew our names," Justin told her. "Dad, how could . . . ?"

But Dad was already climbing in the car. "Kids, you know there are no longer Indian chiefs! Now let's get a move on or it will be dark before we get there!"

"Dad!" Jenny demanded as they piled into the back seat. "Weren't you even worried about us?"

Dad's hazel eyes twinkled, but he answered calmly, "I knew you were safe."

"Never mind," Justin interrupted as the sound of an infuriated kitten came from his twin. "What matters is that we're on the reservation now. So tell us about the place—and this John McCloud."

"Yeah, we've been patient long enough," echoed Jenny. "So what's all the mystery?"

"Hey, can't you two wait just ten more minutes until we get to Rocky Creek?" Dad glanced back at the twins, took in the stubborn set of both chins, then threw up a hand in surrender.

"Okay, you win! And there's no mystery. John was one of my students back when I was still doing my master's degree and teaching undergraduate courses to pay for it. You two were just learning to crawl, right, Helen?"

"That's right," Mom nodded. "John was studying to be a lawyer, and he was a long way from home. You brought him home to supper one night. I still don't know how you got to be such friends because you were always arguing."

Dad shook his head. "John was probably the most brilliant student I ever had. But he thought I was crazy because I was a Christian. He spent hours trying to convince me that no God would concern himself about every single, unimportant little human being on the earth."

"Still, he kept coming around," Mom went on. "Maybe just for a hot, cooked meal at the beginning, but John admired Dad even if he didn't agree. In the end, John was the one convinced! He received Jesus Christ as his personal Savior. He eventually graduated at the top of his class and opened a law practice in California."

"So what happened then?" Justin demanded. "How did he end up on an Indian reservation?"

"I'm not really sure," Mom said. "He was doing well in California. Then about a year ago, he wrote that he was giving up his practice to work as a missionary here on the reservation. You see, he's originally from Montana. In fact, he's a distant cousin of mine."

"Very distant!" Dad threw Mom an amused glance, and Justin wondered what was so funny. "Actually, your mom has relatives all over Montana—even on the reservation!"

"Really!" Justin leaned forward, his hazel eyes sparking with excitement. "You mean, Indians?"

Mom nodded. "My grandfather—your great-grandfather—was a member of this very reservation. *His* mother was a full-blooded Cree. My family moved from Montana before I started school so I never really knew much about that side of the family."

"Cool!" Justin did some mental arithmetic. "That means we're one-sixteenth Indian! So *that's* where you and Jenny get the dark hair and eyes!" He eyed Jenny's golden tan with disgust. "And no sunburn."

Mom laughed. "Maybe, but our French, Irish, and Welsh ancestors had dark hair, too."

"And *our* gorgeous auburn curls might come from those Scandinavian ancestors." Dad patted his carrot-hued hair. "Or maybe from the Scottish—or the Anglo-Saxon, the Danish, or the German!"

"Wow! Do we really come from all those countries?" asked Jenny.

"Sure! And a few more. I guess our family qualifies as just plain all-American."

Dad braked for a drove of cattle that crossed the road up

ahead. A rider on a small, spotted pony was urging the stragglers up the bank. The rider looked a little older than the twins—maybe in his late teens—and could have been any ordinary cowboy, except for the black braid down his back.

Another real Indian! Justin watched in fascination as the cowboy turned an escaping heifer and forced it onto the road. The last of the cattle headed down the opposite bank. Dad rolled down his window and waved, but the rider just stared. Justin thought he saw hostility in those dark eyes before the rider turned his spotted pony and broke into a gallop.

"Well!" Justin burst out. "People sure aren't friendly around here! Just like that guy by the mesa, remember Jenny?"

At last, their car pulled up to a wood-frame church, once painted white, but now weathered and gray. Beside the church was a tiny parsonage built of weathered planks. But Justin was only interested in the tall, dark brown horse that stood tethered to one post of the steep-roofed porch.

"This is it—the Indian Bible Mission!" announced Dad.

Justin tumbled out before the car even stopped and headed for the horse—a beautiful stallion with the long legs and sleek lines of a quarter horse. The animal stood still, its only movement the slow swish-swish of its tail, but its sides were sweaty and lathered. It had been ridden hard—and recently!

Jenny appeared at Justin's elbow and ran a hand over the long, braided mane, then stroked the silky nose. "It's the prettiest horse I've ever seen!"

"Pretty!" Justin snorted. He fingered the brightly colored, woven blanket that alone served as a saddle. "I'll bet it's fast!"

"Rff! Rff! Rff!!" A small tan-and-black dog of no particular breed bounded up and dashed beneath the horse, barking frantically. The horse didn't flinch, but the twins scrambled for the porch. The dog followed and nipped at their heels. Suddenly the screen door banged open.

"Down, White Tail!" a deep voice commanded. "Down!"

The dog dropped to the ground, and its white-tipped tail began to wag. They both breathed a joint sigh of relief and turned to thank their rescuer. But their words froze on their lips as they both stared at the tall man in the doorway. His feathered headdress touched the top of the door frame.

"That's the . . ." "How did you get . . ." Justin and Jenny chorused as they stared at each other, then back again at the tall Indian. Justin could read no expression on the still, bronzed face, but somehow he sensed a twinkle behind the dark eyes. Then he heard quick steps on the porch, and his parents came up behind him.

"Justin . . . Jenny!" Dad boomed, "I'd like to introduce our friend, John McCloud."

Justin was still staring, but Jenny whirled around to her father with indignation. "Dad, why didn't you tell us—?"

"That I'm an Indian?" White teeth flashed in a sudden smile as John McCloud stepped aside and motioned the Parkers through the screen door. "Your father never outgrows his little jokes—do you, Ron?"

Dad looked pleased with his surprise. One eyebrow went up as he eyed John McCloud's feathered headdress. "Looks like I'm not the only one who likes a joke."

Snapping his mouth shut, Justin followed his parents and sister into a small living room. Once inside, John McCloud lifted off the headdress. The long braids came off as well, uncovering dark hair clipped close. He smiled again as Justin and Jenny exchanged a glance of astonishment. "What your Dad means is that I'm not really a chief! This outfit is for Indian Days next week—that's the big event of the year here. We were practicing a riding exhibition when someone rode out to say they'd seen a dark green SUV broken down a few miles down the road. I recognized your description and rode over. Ron was concerned you two might be lost, so I tracked you down. When I saw your faces on that mound, well, I couldn't resist."

"But—how did you disappear like that?" Jenny demanded.

The dark eyes twinkled. "Indian trade secret." His teeth flashed again at the twins' expression. "Now, if you'll excuse me for a moment, I'll change. Then I can help you unload."

Jenny whirled around as he left, hands on her hips. "OK, Dad, I'll admit it! You really had us fooled this time—both of you!"

John McCloud soon returned, dressed in jeans and a checked shirt. He helped the Parkers unload the SUV, then all five crowded around a table in the kitchen for a pot of the spiciest chili Justin and Jenny had ever tasted. Their eyes watered, but both insisted on a second bowl.

"Uh . . . Mr. McCloud?" Jenny set down her spoon. "Dad says you're related to us—kind of a cousin, right?"

"That's right!" John nodded. "Your great-grandfather and my great-grandmother were siblings. I guess that makes us cousins— of sorts!"

Jenny leaned forward. "Does that mean we're members of your tribe?"

He laughed. "Well, officially you're supposed to be one-fourth

Cree. But I'd say anyone whose great-grandfather was born on this reservation deserves an honorary membership!"

Dad pushed back his empty bowl. "That was great, John! Your chili's gotten even better in the last twelve years! So bring us up to date. It was a real surprise to us when you wrote that you were back on the reservation. What happened to that thriving law practice?"

John McCloud grinned across the table. "Actually, you and Helen had a hand in that. You were always encouraging me to study the Bible. So I started taking some classes. I never planned to let my studies interfere with my practice. But the more I studied, the more I began to see that my people, too, needed to hear of God and His love. I knew God was calling me back to my own people." His dark face was suddenly sober. "Though it hasn't been easy . . . especially lately."

"You mentioned in your last letter that there'd been some problems," Dad said with concern. "What's the situation?"

"Well, let's just say that if Philip Dumont has his way, I won't be welcome on the reservation much longer!"

"Who's Philip Dumont?" Dad raised an eyebrow.

"It's a long story. I'm afraid you'll find out more than you'd like to know about him if you stick around a few days." John pushed back his chair and stood up. "But enough of my problems!"

He glanced at Justin and Jenny. "The tribe runs a riding stable. Would you like a ride around the reservation to shake down that chili?"

Justin burst from his chair. "You bet! That sounds great!"

Chapter Three

A FRANTIC RIDE

John McCloud led his horse as they walked over to a long, low stable. Mom had decided to pass on the horse ride, but Dad came along. Justin and Jenny both walked on ahead, excited about the opportunity to ride. When they reached the stable yard, a small girl pedaled by on a rusty metal trike.

"Hi, Sky Teacher!" she shouted as she streaked across their path.

"Hi, Clara!" John called back, as she disappeared in a cloud of dust around the side of the building. He turned to the Parkers. "Among the Cree people, you not only have the name you are born with but also an Indian name you are given or choose when you grow up. It's supposed to tell something about you. My Indian name is Sky Teacher—because I'm always talking about God and heaven."

He smiled down at them. "If you two are going to be honorary members of this reservation, you'll have to call me Sky Teacher like the rest of the tribe." He stopped to speak to the stable manager—the little girl's father.

Justin paused to admire a brown-and-white Appaloosa. Justin and Jenny both knew the basics of riding from summer camps, but they had never saddled a horse. Fortunately, Dad had a little more experience, and it didn't take him long to saddle a tall roan gelding, but Sky Teacher insisted Justin and Jenny try for themselves. He coached Justin as he struggled to fasten the heavy leather straps around the belly of the Appaloosa. Dad helped Jenny, then showed her how to settle the bit in her pinto mare's mouth.

They led their horses to the road, then clambered into the saddles. Sky Teacher adjusted their stirrups, then vaulted to the back of his big, dark brown quarter horse. He grinned as he caught Justin's half-envious stare.

"You like Dark Cloud? Maybe you'd like to ride him sometime." He patted the horse. "Bareback, of course! Dark Cloud doesn't like saddles."

West of the church lay unbroken prairie. But Sky Teacher turned in the other direction and led them past the stable and down the gravel road. The horses all broke into an easy trot. After a few minutes, the gravel turned into pavement, and Jenny kneed her pinto mare up beside Dark Cloud.

"Mr. Mc—uh . . . I mean, Sky Teacher." She waved her arm toward the neat rows of mobile homes and small, wood-frame houses. "Is this *really* Rocky Creek?"

Sky Teacher laughed. "What did you expect? Tepees?"

He turned Dark Cloud off the road into a wide lot filled with rusted-out cars and discarded machinery. "Rocky Creek is our biggest settlement with a population of about six hundred. We have fifteen hundred tribal members scattered around the reservation and about fifteen hundred living off the reservation."

"Do they speak mostly English?" asked Dad.

"A few of the old-timers speak only Cree, but the younger tribal members all learn English in school. Most probably speak more English than Cree." Sky Teacher nodded toward a two-story brick building with a large, fenced-in yard. A faded sign read: Big Sky Elementary. "The reservation school only goes to sixth grade. The government does provide busing to a high school in a nearby town, but a lot of kids drop out rather than leave the reservation. I've been working with the tribal council to get a high school here."

Justin and Jenny fell back, leaving the two men to talk side by side. Justin glanced around. There was something odd about this place—something he couldn't put his finger on. The quiet streets looked like any other small town—maybe a little more shabby and run-down than most.

"This place is weird!" Jenny burst out, echoing his thoughts. "I wonder if it's always this dead."

"That's it!" Justin snapped his fingers. "There aren't any people!"

He glanced up and down the street. The summer evening would stay light until almost ten o'clock, but there were no children playing outside. The porches were empty, and there were no sounds of TV, stereo, or voices.

"Hey look!" Jenny pulled her horse to a stop. "There's someone!"

Justin swiveled in his saddle. A rider on a small, spotted pony came up behind them. Long, dark hair streamed out in the breeze, but as the pony drew closer, Justin saw that the rider was a young man, not a girl. "Hey, that's the cowboy we saw on the road!"

The two men turned at the sound of approaching hoof beats. Sky Teacher raised his hand in greeting as the spotted pony drew even with the other horses. "Good to see you, Bear Paw! Missed you at Bible study last week."

The young rider acknowledged Sky Teacher's greeting with a curt nod, but his face turned sullen as he looked at the visitors. He slapped his pony on the rear and broke into a gallop. Sky Teacher turned back to the Parkers.

"I'm sorry about that! George Bear Paw's a good kid, but he's going through a rough patch right . . ." He cocked his head slightly in concentration.

"What is it?" Dad asked, leaning forward to listen. Justin heard nothing at first, but then picked up the low, distant rumble. *Probably just thunder.* But then, there wasn't a cloud in the sky!

"Come!" Sky Teacher kneed Dark Cloud in the same direction that Bear Paw had disappeared. Dad followed with Justin and Jenny close behind. As they trotted down the street, the low rumble grew into an odd, uneven pounding. It wasn't long before Justin heard shouts and a wild cheering. The noise reached a peak as they turned a corner and came out on the edge of a wide stretch of lawn.

Across the lawn, a huge American flag flapped lazily above a sign that read: Big Sky Community Center. The big, square building was bright with strange, geometric designs and abstract paintings of Indian warriors. Jenny leaned over to her brother. "Here are your missing people!"

Justin nodded. A crowd of all ages was gathered. He could easily see what attracted the mass of people—a platform thrown together of planks and bricks. A dozen men dressed in fringed buckskins circled a huge drum in the center.

"NARC activists." Sky Teacher frowned as he moved closer.

A young Indian stepped to the platform. Justin looked at the large, gold medallion around his neck. The initials NARC were inscribed across it.

"The Great Spirit sent me a vision last night." The young Indian raised his voice above the beat of the drum. "From the top of the mesa I saw Chief Thunderbird ride through the night across Death Canyon. His spirit was angry because we have not preserved the sacred lands of our ancestors."

An excited murmur drowned out the speaker's next words, and Justin turned to study the other men on the platform. They also wore the NARC emblem. And unlike the short-haired men in the crowd of spectators, these had their hair tied back in pony tails or braids. Justin leaned forward to see better. One man on the platform didn't look like an Indian at all! His clipped hair under his feathered hat was brown rather than black, and his features were only slightly tanned. He nodded to a drummer, a stocky Indian, whose head was shaved except for a black strip down the middle that ended in a long braid, and the drumming stopped. Then the brown-haired man stepped forward to speak.

"You have heard from your warriors, those who have seen the visions of the old ones in Death Canyon," he shouted. "The spirits of our ancestors are calling us to return to the ways of our ancestors—to the worship of the ancient ones. We must turn our backs on the call of the white man's world to tear up our sacred lands. We must fight against those who are more concerned with money than the protection of our land!"

Jenny nudged her pinto up beside the Appaloosa. "Is this guy for real?"

"Yeah, he sounds like an old movie!" Justin agreed, but he noticed many of the tribal members nodding in agreement.

"Hey, psst!" Jenny's urgent whisper brought Justin around. She nodded toward Sky Teacher. He was backing Dark Cloud away from the other horses. Wheeling around, he kicked him into a gallop along the outside of the crowd. Justin and Jenny kneed their horses to follow.

Sky Teacher was near the front of the crowd by the time they caught him. Edging Dark Cloud close to the platform, he suddenly called out, "Mr. Dumont, since when has Death Canyon ever been considered sacred to the Indian people? And these visions your followers have seen—would they have something to do with that petition you've been circulating to prevent mineral exploration in the Death Canyon area?"

The activist leader turned in anger, his footsteps sounded loudly above the sudden silence of the crowd as he walked across the platform. Justin kneed his Appaloosa next to Dark Cloud and eyed this man with new interest. *So this is the Philip Dumont who is trying to run Sky Teacher off the reservation!* He grinned to himself. Those high-heeled black boots sure looked funny with that Indian outfit!

Philip Dumont glared at Sky Teacher, then turned back to the crowd. He raised his arms in a dramatic gesture. "The Great Spirit has given the land to the Indian people to honor and preserve. Will we rip up our land looking for wealth for others to enjoy? Will money ever make up for the exploitation of our resources and the destruction of our la . . ."

He broke off in a cough. As he grabbed a glass of water from one of his followers, Sky Teacher said dryly, "We're *all* interested in protecting our environment, Mr. Dumont. But the needs of this reservation must be considered, too. We need more jobs here—a better education for our young people—things that mineral royalties could give us. Mineral development does not necessarily destroy the land. Take natural gas, for instance. It's clean and—"

"And who are you, Sky Teacher, to speak of what is best for the Indian people?" Philip Dumont threw the empty glass to the platform with a shattering crash. "It is *you* who brought the anger of the spirits upon this land—you who left the ways of our ancestors and went running after the white man's God. You are a traitor to your own people!"

His voice rose to a high-pitched scream. His followers pushed to the edge of the platform, shouting and waving their fists, and an angry rumble swept through the crowd. The Appaloosa snorted and sidestepped as the mass of people pressed in around the horses. Justin held the reins tightly, studying the faces of the crowd. Were they agreeing with Mr. Dumont or defending Sky Teacher?

Nearby, Jenny, too, held tight to her reins as her horse reacted to the jostling crowd. But Dark Cloud remained motionless, his nostrils flared only slightly. On his back, Sky Teacher sat tall and straight, his bronze face expressionless as he held the big horse steady.

He really looks like an Indian chief! Justin thought. Even in jeans, Sky Teacher had the same look that he'd seen in one of his history books—a wise old chieftain facing an enemy attack with calm strength and courage.

The shouting dwindled. Justin twisted in his saddle to see a path being cleared for an elderly man whose shoulder-length black hair was touched with gray. His English was slow but clear as he commanded, "Enough of this, Mr. Dumont!"

He stepped carefully onto the platform and raised a hand for silence. "I am not a Christian, but the Christian missionaries have always been the first to help our people. Sky Teacher is one of the finest young leaders to come out of our tribe in many years. Since his return to the reservation, he has worked hard to bring better education to our young people. He has helped those of us on the tribal council many times with legal advice. He is a loyal son of his people."

Angry mutters gave way to nods of agreement, and Sky Teacher turned to face the listening tribal members and said, "You have heard me say this before, but I must repeat it again and again." His quiet tones carried to the edge of the crowd as he continued. "God is not just the God of the Europeans or of any other single group of people. God created and loves all mankind, and He sent His Son, Jesus Christ, to bring salvation to all men of every people."

Way to go, Sky Teacher! Justin threw a triumphant glance at the group of men on the platform. But he caught his breath as his gaze fell on the NARC leader. Philip Dumont glared down at Sky Teacher, his face twisted with unmasked hatred! He gave a slight nod to the stocky Indian with the shaved head. His follower silently stepped to the side of the platform and raised his arm. Justin caught sight of the heavy stone in his fist.

"Sky Teacher! Watch out!" Justin shoved his Appaloosa sideways against the big quarter horse just as the stocky Indian released the rock. He heard it whistle past Sky Teacher's head, missing him only by inches. It landed with a loud thud somewhere behind them.

A startled scream sounded, and Justin realized where the heavy stone had landed! Jenny's startled pinto reared, its front legs lashing out. She grabbed for the saddle horn, her face white and frightened. Holding tight to the saddle, she leaned forward and spoke soothing words to the little mare. But the pinto, already spooked by the pressing crowd, refused to be calmed.

More screams escaped from the bystanders as they scrambled away from the flying hooves, holding onto small children, shielding elders. A man in a plaid shirt grabbed for the reins, and the pinto dropped stiff-legged to the ground. But before Justin could let out a sigh of relief, Jenny's horse broke away from the man's grip, whipped its head around, and tore off into a panicked gallop. The frightened little mare headed for the open prairie behind the community center, Jenny clinging desperately to the back of the runaway horse!

Chapter Four

A SHOCKING DISCOVERY

Justin worked the Appaloosa through the scattering crowd until he was in the clear, then kneed the horse to a gallop and headed after Jenny. Within seconds, Dark Cloud flashed past him with Sky Teacher low on his neck. *Just let her hold on until Sky Teacher gets there!* he prayed as he galloped after the other two horses.

Hoofbeats pounded from behind, and Justin glanced back to see his father urge the roan to a faster gallop. Dad's face was grim as he slowly pulled even with Justin, and the roan and Appaloosa pounded on side by side. The horses were going so fast that Justin began to wonder if *he* would be the one to fall off, but he didn't dare slow down. Ahead of him, Sky Teacher was closing in on the runaway mare; his quarter horse's strong slim legs seemed to fly as he inched closer to Jenny.

Justin could see Jenny crouched low in the saddle, clinging to the saddle horn with both hands, the reins flapping loosely on the mare's neck. Then Dark Cloud was racing neck and neck with the frightened pinto.

She's going to make it! Justin thought. But just as he released a sigh of relief, the pinto caught its front hoof in a small burrow and stumbled. Instantly the mare was back on its feet, but Jenny had lost her grip on the saddle horn and was sliding helplessly off the saddle!

Then in that same split second, Justin saw something he had thought possible only in a movie. Sky Teacher had edged his horse so close that the two animals were almost touching. Leaning over, he plucked Jenny up just as she slid from the saddle. He lifted her up in front of him, then grabbed the mare's harness and yanked her to a halt. By the time Dad and Justin galloped up, he had already dismounted and was calming the lathered animal.

Dad swung down from his horse and reached Jenny in two quick strides. "Jenny, are you all right?"

She held a rumpled bandana to her bleeding nose, but managed a smile. "I'm okay! Just scared out of my wits is all!"

"When I saw that horse rear . . ." Dad cleared his throat, then turned to Sky Teacher. "I don't know how to thank you, John!"

"Yeah, you were awesome! I never saw anyone ride like that!" Justin patted Dark Cloud. "You too, Dark Cloud! You must be the fastest horse in Montana!" The big quarter horse tossed its head and stamped a hoof as though eager to race again.

On their way back to the community center, they saw Philip Dumont roar past in a new white pickup. The big drum was packed in the back. At the center, most of the crowd were gone, but the elderly man who had defended Sky Teacher walked up to them. Sky Teacher swung down from his horse and said quietly, "I thank you, Robert Windy Boy."

The old man looked at him gravely. "I follow the spirits of my ancestors, Sky Teacher, but I know you work only for the good of our people." He turned and walked away.

"Who was that old man, Sky Teacher?" asked Jenny. "Is he someone important? I mean—the way everyone listened to him!"

"That's Robert Windy Boy. He's chairman of the tribal council and one of the wisest elders of our tribe."

Dad glanced back toward the abandoned platform. "I can see now what kind of trouble this Dumont's been causing you. But I still don't understand what he's doing here on the reservation! Is he a member of the tribe?"

"No, he isn't. Though from his speeches you'd think he was the only one interested in the well-being of this reservation! Philip Dumont showed up here about two months ago with a band of his followers, members of a radical Indian rights group called Native American Revolutionary Confederation, or NARC. They recruited a few local followers and have been stirring up the reservation ever since, calling for the people to return to the ways of our ancestors, including the ancient Indian spirit worship."

Sky Teacher kept the horses to a slow amble as he went on, "Most of the tribe was pretty suspicious when I came back as a missionary, but I've worked hard to develop a good relationship between the tribe and the church. Like Robert Windy Boy said, I've been able to offer legal advice to the tribal council and use my law training to lobby for educational grants for the tribe. But Philip Dumont and his followers are doing their best to turn the tribe against me . . . *and* the Indian Bible Mission. I'm afraid they've succeeded with much of the younger generation."

"Like Bear Paw?"

Sky Teacher nodded. "Bear Paw was a faithful member of one of my Bible studies. But he doesn't come much since he started following Philip Dumont around."

Dad raised an eyebrow. "So . . . what does all this have to do with that Death Canyon area you two mentioned?"

"I'm not too sure of *that* myself," Sky Teacher answered dryly. "The Death Canyon area is part of a land deal the tribe made about a year ago—ten thousand acres adjoining the present reservation. It was the first legal contract I ever drew up for the tribe. It's undeveloped prairie, but the tribal council had hopes the land might hold natural resources that could benefit the tribe."

"Mineral resources, you mean. Your last letter said you hoped to get my brother Pete up here to check out the possibilities of oil or gas or some other kind of mineral here on the reservation."

"Yes, we *had* hoped to get Pete up here," Sky Teacher agreed. "A lot of mineral resources have been discovered across Montana in the last few years. They've brought new jobs and prosperity to several of the other reservations. A geological survey done here on the reservation a few years back came up negative, but we'd hoped something might turn up on this new land. I'm no expert, but the geology—especially in the Death Canyon area—is very similar to other regions where oil and gas have been found."

"And those difficulties you mentioned earlier, is that where Philip Dumont comes in?"

"Dumont is lobbying to prevent any exploration or mineral development on the new land. He claims to be the president of some Indian Historical Foundation whose goal is to preserve ancient sacred grounds and historical sites of the Indian people. He seems to have developed a special interest in the Death Canyon area."

So far, Justin and Jenny had quietly listened to the two men, but as Sky Teacher finished, Jenny jumped in.

"You mean, Death Canyon is really an Indian sacred ground?"

Sky Teacher's teeth flashed in the growing dusk. "To be honest, Jenny, I'd never heard any of those claims about Death Canyon until the last few months, and I grew up here. There *was* some old story about it being a place of bad luck. But folks don't stay away from there because they think it's some ancient Indian sacred ground. It just happens to be the most desolate piece of country around here—no grazing or anything else—not to mention that the only way there is on foot or horseback."

"I'll bet it'd be fun to explore!" Justin's hazel eyes glowed with enthusiasm. "Do you think we could go up there—to Death Canyon, I mean?"

"I couldn't even tell you which of those gorges *is* Death Canyon! But I'm going to check out that area for myself tomorrow morning. If you kids are up in time, you're welcome to ride along."

There was only one guest bedroom in the tiny parsonage, so Justin and Jenny spread out sleeping bags in a Sunday school room next door. Justin was crawling into his sleeping bag when a high-pitched cry pierced the night.

"What was that!" Jenny sat straight up in her sleeping bag. The twins listened as a throbbing, syncopated rhythm joined the eerie rise and fall of the strange, wordless singing.

"It's just Indian drums," Justin said with relief.

By the next morning, Justin's sunburn had eased, but he slathered well with sunscreen before the twins hurried over to the parsonage. Sky Teacher was already in the kitchen. He dropped a twisted length of bread dough into a cast iron pot on the gas stove. Justin's stomach rumbled at the crackle of sizzling fat. Jenny leaned over the pot. "Hey, that sure smells good! What is it?"

"Our special kind of fry bread. If you're going to be an honorary member of this tribe, you'll have to learn to make it." Sky Teacher placed a plate of the steaming browned dough on the table, then added a pitcher of milk and a bowl of dark, spicy-smelling honey. "I told your parents to sleep as late as they wanted." Sky Teacher bowed his head in a short grace, then piled their plates high with the fried bread.

"Boy this honey's great—kind of like cinnamon and cloves!" Justin mumbled as he wiped his mouth after the last chewy bite.

"That's sagebrush honey from our own tribal hives. The tourists always like it!" Getting to his feet, Sky Teacher clapped on a broad-brimmed tan hat. "Now if either of you wants to ride with me to Death Canyon," he nodded toward a row of broad-brimmed hats that hung on pegs by the back door, "grab a hat and let's go!"

They found it much easier to saddle their horses this time. As they led the horses from the stable, Sky Teacher's small tan-and-black dog bounded around the house, its entire rear wagging with excitement. "White Tail, stay!" he ordered sternly. "This is too far for you to come."

The little dog reluctantly returned to the house. Sky Teacher led them across the gravel road that ran in front of the church. A breeze rustled through the grass, but the cloudless blue sky overhead promised another hot day.

"This is the boundary of the old reservation," explained Sky Teacher as they trotted out onto the prairie. He pointed out the tableland they had seen the day before, now barely visible above the horizon. "Everything from here to the other side of that mesa is part of the land the tribe bought last year."

"Who owned it all before?" asked Jenny.

"No one, really—just the federal government."

They approached the mesa. Justin recognized the area where they'd gotten lost the day before. Sky Teacher turned Dark Cloud to ride in the shadow of the mesa wall. Jogging single file behind the other two, Justin stared up at the mesa looming high above his head. Layers of differently colored rock gave the walls a striped look—like a layered birthday cake. *Hey, this is where that guy with the shovel and knapsack was riding yesterday!* he realized suddenly.

They soon left behind the shade of the mesa, and the slope of the land began to rise. The short prairie grass and sagebrush gave way to rock and tumbled boulders. Sky Teacher pulled up his horse. "Well, kids, this should be the right area. Now let's see if we can find Death Canyon."

Justin reined in beside Dark Cloud. The country was desolate, just as Sky Teacher had told them. A high cliff still some miles away stretched from east to west as far as he could see. From its flat top, the prairie grasses continued to a distant range of hills. But between the three riders and the cliff, the landscape was carved into dozens of gullies and ravines. No wonder Sky Teacher couldn't tell which one was Death Canyon!

Leaning over Dark Cloud's neck, Sky Teacher scanned the ground ahead of him. "It looks like there's been a couple of other riders in here lately. I'd say if we follow these tracks, they're bound to lead us to Death Canyon."

The sun was now high overhead. It blazed from the stony

ground and limestone walls of the canyon. Justin tilted his cowboy hat over his face as he studied the hard-baked earth. There was no sign *he* could see of other riders! Glancing up, he saw that the other two horses were already threading down into a shallow gully. He kicked the Appaloosa into a trot.

The gully gradually deepened into a ravine. As Sky Teacher paused to study the ground again, Justin nudged his horse past the other two, and continued on into the ravine. It gradually narrowed until it was only wide enough for one horse, and the rock walls grew higher, casting tall shadows, which felt chilly after the heat of the open prairie.

Then the ravine widened again into sunshine and came to an abrupt end. Up ahead, Justin noticed a shallow opening in the limestone wall, probably carved by the spring floods. Inside—propped up against the back wall as though taking a rest from the heat—was a human skeleton. Cold fingers crept up Justin's spine as he met its black, empty gaze.

Chapter Five

DEATH CANYON

"Justin, are you all right?" Sky Teacher's sharp call echoed down the ravine.

Now how did he know? Justin wondered. *I didn't even make a sound.* But he called back. "I'm fine, but you'd better come and see this!"

The shallow cave was just high enough to be easily seen from horseback. Justin nudged the Appaloosa closer, and the skeleton's cold, dark stare dissolved into two dusty holes in a dirt-stained skull. *See, it's just a bunch of old bones!* he told himself firmly. Then his gaze sharpened. Those were freshly dug clumps of dirt clinging to the long, bleached bones! That skeleton couldn't have been sitting here long. But where had it come from?

Glancing around, Justin saw for the first time that the ravine didn't actually end here at the shallow cave. Instead, it made a sharp right turn and continued a short distance to the end— not another limestone wall, but the bright sunshine of open ground. Justin's hazel eyes narrowed as he noticed a clump of fresh dirt a few feet away—then another and another! The dirt clods traced a clear trail toward the turn in the ravine.

The other two horses clattered up behind him. Jenny gave a

startled gasp at the sight of the skeleton. Sky Teacher studied the skeleton for a few moments, then reached into the cave and pried out a small object that had lodged itself between the hip joints. He turned it over in his hand. "Hmm! Looks like this guy's been around a long time, a hundred years, anyway! Let's see . . . we've got a male about five-foot-eight—that was pretty tall back then! He was young *and* fairly healthy. I wonder what killed him! There's no signs of a bullet wound or any other cause of death."

Justin craned to see. "How can you tell how old he was when he died?"

"See these teeth? This guy's still got a full set! Teeth didn't last long back when they had no dentists."

Sky Teacher brushed a clump of fresh dirt from a leg bone, then swung down from Dark Cloud to study the ground. Justin was startled at the sudden grim note in his voice. "This skeleton didn't come from around here! It was carried here by a man about 180 pounds, five foot eleven, wearing Indian clothing and high-heeled boots."

Justin knit his eyebrows together. Why did that description sound familiar?

Jenny swung down beside Sky Teacher and examined the dusty ravine floor with puzzled eyes. "How can you tell all that? I don't see anything!"

"See that?" Sky Teacher squatted and pointed out the horseshoe-shaped print of a boot heel. "That boot's about a size ten. The stride tells me it's a man, and you can see how much he weighs by the depth of the track. He walks like a city slicker, so he isn't from the reservation. But take a look at this!" He pointed out some faint markings on the ledge where the skeleton was sitting. "These were made by a leather fringe, like on that outfit I wore yesterday. Whoever put this skeleton here brushed his sleeve through the dirt when he arranged the bones."

"But why would anyone want to stick a skeleton here?" Jenny asked.

"My guess is that someone's trying to scare off any stray hikers." Sky Teacher nodded toward the skeleton. "That thing would sure keep any tribal members out of here! The Indian people don't believe in poking around the dead."

"Me either!" Jenny agreed with a shudder. She studied the skeleton again, then looked sideways at the Indian missionary. "Sky Teacher, really—how did you disappear like that yesterday? Was it really some Indian secret?"

Sky Teacher grinned. "That Indian secret is really just a matter of learning to move quietly and invisibly. When you turned around, I just dropped to the ground behind that ridge. I waited for you to leave, then walked back to my horse and rode cross-country to get home before you arrived."

It sounded simple, but Justin decided that it probably wasn't as easy as it seemed. Leaving the other two still searching the ground, he rode on ahead. Heat struck like a blow as the ravine opened onto a flat, barren plateau. Across the plateau, Justin spotted the high cliff they had seen from the mesa, now less than a quarter mile ahead.

He kicked his horse into a gallop, but he had covered only a few hundred yards when the Appaloosa stopped so suddenly that Justin had to grab the saddle horn to keep from flying over the horse's neck. He shuddered when he looked down to see the ground in front of him break away into a long, sheer drop-off.

Backing the horse carefully away from the edge, Justin slid down from the saddle. The canyon was several hundred feet long and less than a hundred feet wide. Justin dropped flat on his stomach and peered cautiously over the edge.

The canyon wall fell straight down for some distance before angling outward in a steep slope that broke off at a ledge only a few feet wide. On the ledge was a mound of freshly dug earth, with a few loose clumps scattered down the canyon edge. So this was where the skeleton had come from! *But why did the man die on that ledge? Why didn't he climb the rest of the way up? What killed him?* Justin inspected the canyon wall. Its rough face offered plenty of footholds. He swung a foot over the edge.

"What are you doing here, boy? Don't you know this land is sacred to the Indian people?"

Justin froze as a shadow fell across him. He eased his foot back onto solid ground and raised his head. His heart raced as he recognized the man who glared down at him from the back of a dappled gray horse. It was the NARC leader, Philip Dumont.

Justin scrambled to his feet and backed away. But before he could reach his horse, Philip Dumont dismounted and walked rapidly toward him.

"*He* died because he angered the spirits who guard this sacred ground," Dumont said coldly glancing over the edge at the signs of recent digging below. Justin's eyes opened wide. *How does he know about the skeleton?*

"*He* thought to escape, but he didn't make it. And you'll die, too, if you set foot in Death Canyon!"

Death Canyon! Justin stared down into the canyon depths. The deep gorge did look uninviting with its narrow, bleached-white floor with no hint of vegetation. But he wasn't about to admit anything to this man. He shrugged. "It looks like any other canyon to me!"

"Does it?" Philip Dumont grabbed him by the arm and pointed down into the hollow at the base of the cliff. A dead deer lay in the shadow of the tumbled boulders, a vulture feeding upon the carcass. Justin angrily yanked his arm free and watched as the vulture slowly spread its wings and gave a feeble flap. Then the bird drooped over as though it were sick. Justin noticed another half-decayed animal carcass nearby and scattered piles of what must be bones. It did look strange.

"You see! It is a place of the spirits—a place of death." Philip Dumont lowered his voice in a dramatic hiss. "The spirits will give death to anyone who disturbs the rest of Death Canyon!"

"It looks to me like someone already did," a quiet voice broke in. Justin spun around. He let out his breath in a whoosh of relief as he saw Sky Teacher and Jenny.

Philip Dumont turned to face Sky Teacher. "What gives you that idea?"

"Who else weighs about 180 pounds and wears ceremonial Indian dress with high-heeled boots," Sky Teacher answered dryly. "And who else would be out here rooting up remains to prove this is some sacred Indian ground! You brought that skeleton up yesterday afternoon, judging by the trail you left!"

"Don't be ridiculous!" Philip Dumont snapped as he swung back onto the dappled gray horse.

Suddenly Justin remembered. "Hey, yeah! You're the rider we saw yesterday back by the mesa! You were carrying a shovel and a knapsack."

"Yeah, we were lost!" Jenny added indignantly. "You wouldn't answer when we called for help!"

Philip Dumont gave them a cold look. Sky Teacher rode over to the canyon edge and looked down. "What are you up to, Dumont? It's been a hundred years or more since anyone's taken seriously that old legend about Death Canyon being a place of bad luck. The spirits don't seem to have bothered *you* any when you hauled up that skeleton to scare away anyone curious enough to check out the canyon."

Philip Dumont leaned forward on his horse, his tanned features ugly with anger. "The spirits I follow protect me as I bring up evidence for those who still doubt my visions. And even *I* would not descend far into the depths of Death Canyon. But you!" The words hissed through his clenched teeth. "You who left the reservation and the worship of your ancestors. You have angered the spirits! It would be your death to enter Death Canyon!" With an odd look on his face, he waved a fringed arm over the canyon. "You're certainly welcome to try!"

They were interrupted by the heavy thud of hoofbeats. Justin recognized the rider as the stocky Indian with the shaved head who had thrown the rock the night before. Sky Teacher looked from Philip Dumont to the approaching rider, then turned to Justin and Jenny. "Come on. We'd better get you home before your parents think someone's kidnapped you!"

Justin climbed back into his saddle, and the three trotted back across the plateau. "That guy gives me the creeps!" Jenny burst out as soon as they were out of earshot. She hesitated. "What he said back there . . . about Death Canyon . . . that wasn't true, was it?"

Sky Teacher sighed. "Jenny, the Indians have had many places that were considered bad luck or places of death, and often for very good reasons. A water hole might be alkali—poisonous to drink. Or a tepee—maybe even a cave—might be infected with smallpox or some other contagious disease. Once a few people died, our Indian ancestors would avoid such an area, calling it a place of death. Often evil spirits got the blame for unexplained deaths. Maybe such a happening was behind the old legend of Death Canyon. But, like I said before, this is the first I've ever heard of it being some sacred Indian ground!"

When they got back, Sky Teacher took the Parkers on a tour of the reservation, piling into his double cab pickup as the SUV was still out of commission. They started with the small tribal museum. Justin paused in front of an old photo of an Indian chieftain in a feathered headdress. The chieftain sat on the back of a spotted horse, his dark face inscrutable as he stared into the lens of that long-ago camera.

"That's Chief Thunderbird." Sky Teacher walked up behind Justin.

"You mean, the chief those guys saw up in the sky over Death Canyon?" Justin studied the photograph more closely.

"That's what they said!" Sky Teacher said. "Chief Thunderbird was the greatest leader of our tribe. It was he who gathered the remnants of the Cree and brought them here to the reservation."

Next they visited the Big Sky Buffalo Range. Justin and Jenny headed straight for the barbed-wire fence to watch the buffalo that chewed lazily nearby. One massive beast lifted its bearded head, then ambled over to the fence. They stepped back as it rubbed its shaggy back against a wooden post. Satisfied, it gave them a cool stare.

Sky Teacher led them to the edge of a drop-off about fifty feet high. "This was once used as a buffalo jump. The buffalo came through these plains in herds miles across. Back before guns, an entire tribe would work together to stampede a herd over this cliff. One good stampede would supply the tribe for the winter—meat, hides for tepees and clothing, tendons for thread, hooves for glue."

Sky Teacher stared out over the horizon as though still seeing the great herds of buffalo that had once blackened the prairies. "When buffalo hunters came with rifles, they wiped out the herds, and a way of life ended for the Plains Indians. All those hunting and tracking and fighting skills don't help much in today's world. If my people are to survive, we need to learn the skills of *this* world. At the moment, many here on the reservation have lost all hope for the future of our people."

Justin caught a sudden sadness in the black eyes. Now that he knew the tall Indian missionary, he wondered why he'd ever found the bronzed features expressionless. Dad threw a long arm around his friend's shoulders. "John, you know you're doing everything you can!"

"That's right," Mom added gently. "You've given them the only hope there is—faith in Jesus Christ!"

"Yeah, and maybe you'll find those mineral resources you were talking about." Jenny gave Sky Teacher an impulsive hug. "I'll pray about it."

"I will too," Justin added.

"Thanks, friends! And you're right, Helen. The only real hope for my tribe is in Jesus Christ." His somber mood lightened as they started back. He and Dad soon had everyone laughing with their stories of college days. They were almost back to Rocky Creek when Dad leaned over the backseat. "By the way, John, you must be pushing thirty by now! How is it you haven't been snapped up by anyone yet?"

Sky Teacher didn't answer, but dark red tinged his bronze cheekbones. Jenny was quick to sniff out a possible romance. "You *do* have a girlfriend, don't you?"

"Well, actually . . ." Sky Teacher stopped.

"You might as well tell us about her," Mom said with resignation. "You're not going to get any peace until you do."

"Her name is Marie." Sky Teacher kept his deep voice matter-of-fact. "We met in a biblical archeology class. She's Indian, too—half Cree, half Sioux. Marie's been doing her training as a social worker at the University of California."

Dad clapped his friend on the shoulder. "So why don't you bring her out here?"

"Well, I'd planned to go back this last month to ask . . ." Sky Teacher's strong hands tightened on the steering wheel. "How can I ask *any* girl to come out to this situation?"

Loud voices and the beat of a drum interrupted their conversation as they drove into Rocky Creek. Another NARC rally! Outside the Community Center, a white van with *Great Falls News* lettered across the side was pulled up next to the platform. Two men perched on the van with cameras, and on the platform a smartly dressed blonde reporter was thrusting her microphone under Philip Dumont's nose.

"Mr. Dumont, you are trying to prevent mineral exploration on the land the reservation has acquired. Isn't this counterproductive for the Indian people?"

Philip Dumont looked furious as he faced the cameras, but he answered easily enough, "The vision of the spirits has shown me that Death Canyon is an ancient burial ground of my people. The government of this country has laws protecting historical sites of the Indian people from desecration. It is my duty and that of the Indian Historical Foundation to make sure those laws are enforced."

"And these 'visions'—is that all the proof you've got?" The reporter's sarcasm was biting. "Maybe we could drive out there and see this Death Canyon for ourselves!"

"Death Canyon is sacred to the Indian people. It is not to be profaned by outsiders!" Philip Dumont raised both fringed arms high, reminding Justin of an angry bird of prey. Dropping his arms, he spoke quietly, "The spirits have spoken to me. If the tribal council would care to ride out to Death Canyon in the morning, they will find all the proof they need."

As they walked away, Justin asked Sky Teacher, "Do you think Mr. Dumont really believes all that stuff? I mean, he sounds like an actor or something."

Sky Teacher glanced back at the platform with narrowed eyes. "I don't know, Justin. But he's certainly determined to keep development experts and everyone else away from Death Canyon."

Justin and Jenny slept in the Sunday school room again. It was stifling hot, even with the windows open. They tossed and turned on top of their sleeping bags long after the parsonage lights went off. Rolling onto his back, Justin listened lazily to a vehicle moving up the gravel road in front of the church. The engine stopped. It was a long moment before the realization emerged from Justin's drowsy thoughts that the vehicle had never passed the church. Half-asleep, he debated moving for another long moment, but a muffled yelp and the faint thud of footsteps brought him reluctantly to his feet.

Wandering over to the open window, he looked out across the churchyard. He stifled an exclamation. Jenny joined him, whispering, "What is it, Justin?"

"Look!" Justin pointed.

The pickup parked on the road in front of the church showed no lights, but its white paint gleamed in the soft light of an almost-full moon. Jenny gasped as she recognized the man who stood beside the passenger door. It was Philip Dumont.

Chapter Six

GHOST OF CHIEF THUNDERBIRD

The Indian activist climbed into the cab. Then the engine burst into a muffled roar, but the pickup still showed no lights as it moved slowly away.

"What's he doing here at this time of night?" Jenny demanded. "And why is he sneaking around with no headlights?"

"I don't know," Justin answered grimly. "But I'll bet it's something to cause more trouble for Sky Teacher."

Dashing outside, Justin was just in time to see a gleam of white as the pickup turned off at the tribal riding stables a hundred yards down the road. The muffled roar of the motor cut off abruptly.

Jenny was still at the window when he ran back inside. "What are you doing?" she asked in astonishment as he yanked on a pair of jeans.

"Hurry up! Get dressed!"

"Just tell me why I'm doing this in the middle of the night!"

"We gotta see what he's up to! Come on!"

"So what did he want here?" whispered Jenny as she followed Justin out into the moonlit churchyard.

"Maybe he just wanted to make sure we were all asleep," Justin suggested, "before he—well, whatever he's doing!"

Justin and Jenny turned as one to stare across the empty lot that lay between the church and the tribal stable. A gleam of white behind the stable showed where the pickup was parked out of sight of any road traffic. From long practice, they had only to glance at each other to decide what to do next. The moon lit their way as they crept stealthily through the tangled brush that choked the empty lot.

They had just reached the side of the long, wood-frame building when Justin stepped on a dry branch. It cracked with a snap that seemed as loud as a gunshot in the still night. He froze, waiting for some reaction from inside the stable. But if anyone had heard, they obviously didn't consider it worth checking out. He glanced back at his sister, who had frozen in mid-step behind him.

"Watch your step!" he hissed.

"You watch *your* step!" Jenny whispered back. "I can sneak a lot quieter than you can!"

This was true, Justin had to admit as Jenny slipped past him as silently as a ghost—or an Indian. Justin followed her around the corner, trying to keep his own heavier feet quiet. The stable door stood slightly ajar, and a narrow bar of light lay across the ground. The twins looked at each other, then slipped across the stable yard. Jenny placed an eye to the crack while Justin craned to see over her shoulder.

"I'd like to know who called in the press!" A battery-powered lantern set on the stable floor made a circle of light just inside the wide double doors. Philip Dumont was crouched inside that circle, his back to them as he bent over an open briefcase. "I should be sleeping right now, not chasing out to Death Canyon to satisfy the curiosity of a bunch of nosy reporters!"

"Some of the guys got carried away," came an apologetic answer from the long, narrow passageway that ran between the horses' stalls.

The owner of the voice came into view, leading a saddled horse. It was the Indian activist with the shaved head. He had changed his Indian dress for jeans and a sleeveless T-shirt, and he looked a lot more powerful than Justin remembered, with heavy shoulder muscles and bulging biceps. "They actually thought you'd appreciate some news coverage of our great fight to preserve Indian lands."

"We need to keep this on the reservation!" Philip Dumont was lifting out the contents of the briefcase as he spoke. Justin glimpsed an age-blackened rattle carved from some sort of shell and a small circle woven around a square cross before the activist leader stuffed them into a leather saddlebag. "Sky Teacher is causing enough trouble without bringing in outsiders. I'm counting on you, Yellow Dog, to get this back under control. That's what you're paid for, after all!"

"No sweat, boss." Yellow Dog picked up a burlap bag that looked as though it might contain a large bag of flour and slung it behind the horse's saddle. Leaving the horse just outside the circle of light, he headed back toward the stalls.

"I suppose one carefully controlled visit won't hurt!" Philip Dumont lifted out a stone peace pipe like the one they had seen in the museum. Wrapping it in a length of cloth, he placed it carefully in the saddlebag. "In fact, we may be able to turn this to our advantage."

Yellow Dog led another saddled horse out from the stalls. Philip Dumont gave a low, unpleasant chuckle as he threw the leather saddlebag over its back. "They want a sacred burial, we'll give them a sacred burial!"

Picking up the horse's reins, he headed toward the stable doors. Justin and Jenny didn't wait to hear any more. They reached the water trough just as the heavy doors swung open. Throwing themselves to the ground behind the trough, they watched the two men swing into their saddles and ride out of the yard.

It wasn't until the two riders had disappeared into the night that they scrambled to their feet. Jenny yawned. "A sacred burial? What in the world is *that?*"

"I don't know! But I know how we can find out! Come on!"

Vaulting over the water trough, Justin raced across the stable yard. He was lifting the bar that latched the stable door when Jenny caught up to him.

"If you're thinking of doing what I think you're thinking of doing," she lectured, following on his heels as he hurried into the stable, "you're crazy!"

"You don't have to come if you don't want to!" Justin was already opening the stall door. Leading the Appaloosa from its stall, he lifted the heavy saddle to the horse's back. "But I'll bet Sky Teacher would be glad to know what they're up to. Besides, aren't you even a little curious to know why they're sneaking out to Death Canyon at this time of night?"

"A little." Jenny admitted. She yawned and sighed. "All right! If you're going to drag us into another mystery, I'd better go along to keep you out of trouble."

It would be faster, they decided, if they both rode the

Appaloosa. Jenny helped Justin tug the straps tight. But she frowned as he led the horse out of the stable, the clatter of hoof beats sharp against the still night. "They're going to hear us coming a mile away. And I don't think they'll be too happy to see us!"

"Yeah, I know." Justin looked helplessly around the stable yard.

"I've got an idea!" Jenny disappeared into the stable. She came out a moment later with a roll of twine and a large piece of an old blanket that had been used as a cleaning rag. She handed the blanket to Justin. "Here! Cut this into four pieces with your pen knife."

Justin saw instantly what his twin had in mind. "Hey, that's brilliant, Jenny!"

Jenny shrugged, but she looked pleased. "It's just something I read in an old Western. Let's see if it works."

It did. Slipping the thick pieces of cloth under each of the four hooves, they bound them tightly to the narrow legs. When they finally rode across the road, the Appaloosa's hoofbeats were only a muffled thud on the hard ground. Jenny checked the phosphorescent glow of her watch. "They're twenty minutes ahead of us! How are we ever going to find them now?"

"We don't have to," Justin said over his shoulder. "They said they were going to Death Canyon. We'll go straight there!"

"You think you can get us there without getting lost?" Jenny asked doubtfully.

"Sure!" Justin tried to sound confident. They trotted west in the same direction Sky Teacher had led them that morning. Already the church and parsonage had dropped into the night behind them. He pointed to the massive bulk of the mesa looming black against a backdrop of stars. "We just have to ride around the back of the mesa and follow that gully up to the canyon."

A high-pitched howl rose ahead of them. Justin yanked the Appaloosa to a stop. The long wailing cry slowly died away to a yip-yip-yip. But now another howl was rising on his right, then another and another. They were all around them now and growing closer!

"It's wolves!" Jenny clutched Justin tighter around the waist. "Oh, Justin, we'd better go back!"

Justin's own heart was racing, but the Appaloosa trotted on calmly, its ears pricked forward but showing no sign of alarm. Justin gave a shaky laugh. "It's just coyotes! I read somewhere that they sound like they're right next to you when they're really miles away!"

He kicked the Appaloosa into a gallop. A silver moon path lay at their feet. Overhead, strewn from one horizon to the other, the constellations blazed against a blackness undimmed by city lights.

They quickly approached the black bulk of the mesa. The Appaloosa dropped to a trot as they edged along the towering mesa wall. There was no sound but the faint creaking of the saddle and their own quiet breathing. Even the yipping of the coyotes had died away.

Leaving the mesa behind, they rode on until the prairie grasses gave way to the limestone rock that marked the Death Canyon area. Confused, Justin reined in the horse. The light of moon and stars had turned the limestone to ghostly silver, but the ravines and gullies that crisscrossed the landscape were a maze of black lines. Nothing looked as it had during the day! At last he gestured toward one shadowed opening. "That one looks about right."

"How can you tell?" Jenny sounded skeptical. "They all look alike!"

"I can't," Justin said flatly. "But it's as good as any."

He let the Appaloosa pick its own way into the dark mouth of the gully. It was several moments before he noticed a rhythmic clip-clip added to the muffled thud of the horse's hooves. One of their carefully bound foot coverings had worked loose!

Exasperated, he reined the Appaloosa to a quieter walk. The gully deepened into a ravine that soon ended in a stone wall.

Justin glanced around. There was no shallow cave or sharp turn to the right. His heart sank. This was definitely not the right gully and the only way out was back the way they had come. With every delay they were losing any chance of finding out what Philip Dumont and Yellow Dog were doing in Death Canyon in the middle of the night!

But Jenny was sliding down from the horse. "Just leave the horse here," she whispered. "Maybe we can see the canyon from the top."

Grabbing a projection of rock above her head, she started climbing up the stone wall of the ravine. Justin followed her, leaving the Appaloosa's reins trailing on the ground. He discovered it was an easy climb as he felt for footholds in the dark, and in a few short moments, they were both standing on top of the wall.

Jenny gave her brother a triumphant nudge. "There it is!"

The gully they had ridden into was parallel to the one where they'd found the skeleton. And there, far across the moonlit plain, was the slash of darkness that marked Death Canyon.

Justin and Jenny started across the flat rock that separated them from the plateau. After only a few steps, the stamping of hooves and the murmur of nearby voices dropped them to the ground. Side by side, they inched forward on their bellies until they reached the edge of the rock wall that circled the plateau. Cautiously they raised their heads. There was no sign of the men, but two horses stamped impatiently in front of a shadowed opening a few yards to their right. A cave. Stretched across the saddle of one horse was the ghostly outline of a skeleton. Justin and Jenny stared at each other in amazement.

"Isn't that the same . . . ?" Justin gripped his sister's arm hard as her voice rose above a whisper. Someone stepped out of the cave. It was Yellow Dog, and he glanced in their direction. But he strode over to the horses without raising his gaze to the top of the limestone wall. Hoisting the skeleton over his shoulder, he carried it over to the cave. He then opened the leather saddlebag and lifted out the strange collection of artifacts Philip Dumont had packed there. The long stem of the peace pipe glinted in the moonlight as he handed it into the cave.

When Yellow Dog had emptied the leather bag, he slung it back across the saddle. A moment later, Philip Dumont stepped out of the cave. Yellow Dog handed him what looked like a large, pointed paintbrush, and he crawled back inside. Emerging again a few minutes later, he carefully ran the brush across the cave entrance, then over the ground in front of the cave.

"He's brushing out their tracks!" Jenny exclaimed in a whisper. "But why is he leaving all those things in there?"

The two men swung into their saddles. Yellow Dog trotted along the limestone wall in the opposite direction while Philip Dumont cantered across the plateau toward Death Canyon. At the edge of the plateau, he turned and lifted his hand in a curious motion, almost as though he were giving a signal.

"I'll bet it all has something to do with that 'sacred burial' he was talking about," Justin whispered. But Jenny was not listening. Justin felt her stiffen beside him, and he turned to follow her gaze out over the plateau.

A larger-than-life Indian warrior galloped across the black sky above the canyon. The hooves of his spotted pony made no sound, and his long, black hair streamed back in a wind that could not reach them. Colored lights flickered along the warrior's uplifted spear.

The strange apparition appeared solid—nothing like the flat projection of a motion picture. But stars glimmered through the feathered headdress, and Justin could see the face of the cliff right through the rounded body of the spotted horse. It wasn't until the flashing hooves carried the galloping warrior beyond a curve of the limestone wall that he remembered where he had seen that same spotted horse and mounted figure only hours before.

"That's Chief Thunderbird!" he whispered in astonished disbelief. "That was the ghost of Chief Thunderbird!"

Chapter Seven

WHITE TAIL

Justin and Jenny lay motionless on top of the wall. Yellow Dog had returned to Dumont's side, and now the two men were standing at the canyon edge, looking down into its depths and talking. At last, they swung back into their saddles and rode off. Justin and Jenny waited until they disappeared into a shadow in the plateau wall. When the last clatter of hoof beats died away, they sat up. Justin stared out across the now empty night sky.

"That really was Chief Thunderbird!" he repeated incredulously. "He was exactly like the picture in the museum!"

Jenny shook her head in bewilderment. "Sky Teacher thought those activists were lying when they said they saw his spirit out here. But they were telling the truth all the time! Does that mean there really *are* ghosts?"

"Of course not," Justin answered, but his voice trailed off uncertainly.

"Well, I'm not climbing down there in the dark to rummage around that skeleton!" Jenny said firmly. "Let's go!"

Both the twins and the Appaloosa were tired now, and the ride home took far longer than the ride out. When they finally reached the stable, the doors were standing open and a light burned inside. The tall figure of a man was silhouetted against the doorway.

"Do you two know what time it is?" Sky Teacher demanded. "It's 2:30 in the morning! What are you doing out riding at this hour?"

"We saw Philip Dumont. . . . He was outside the parsonage. . . . We followed them to Death Canyon. . . ."

Justin and Jenny's words tumbled over each other. Sky Teacher's stern expression faded as they told him what they had seen.

"We'll talk about this in the morning," he said when they finished. He reached for the Appaloosa's reins. "I'll put up your horse. You two had better get to bed if you're planning on coming to church tomorrow."

Justin had forgotten that the next day was Sunday. It seemed he had just tumbled back into his sleeping bag when an insistent tap at the door woke him up.

"Justin! Jenny!" Mom put her head around the door. "Breakfast will be ready in fifteen minutes."

Justin grabbed his Sunday clothes and hurried over to the parsonage for a shower. He stopped short when he saw Bear Paw standing on the front porch with Sky Teacher.

"I *saw* the vision over Death Canyon last night." Bear Paw's voice was low and intense. "This man Dumont is right! The spirits of our ancestors are calling for our worship. I will not come to your church again."

The young Indian cowboy turned and strode down the path, but not before Justin caught sight of the NARC emblem hanging around his neck.

A sleepy Jenny dragged herself into the parsonage a few minutes later. Over Mom's breakfast of pancakes and sausage, Justin and Jenny told their parents everything that had happened the night before. "It really was Chief Thunderbird—just like they said," Jenny insisted, "except he was as tall as the cliff!"

Dad looked across at Sky Teacher. "There's no doubt they saw something. Could it have been some kind of movie projection?"

Justin shook his head. "It wasn't a picture! He galloped right across the sky! And it was—you know—three-dimensional. Like you could go up and touch him."

Sky Teacher leaned forward. His voice was calm, but Justin saw worry in his eyes. "I don't know what you two saw. But Bear Paw saw the same thing from the top of the mesa last night. And he's not the only one who's fallen for Philip Dumont's talk of spirits and visions."

"Right now, I have a vision of you two doing the dishes," said Dad. "And next time you decide to take a midnight ride, you talk to us first!"

Justin and Jenny made no protest, relieved to get off so easily. They had hung up their dish towels and were heading across the backyard to straighten up the Sunday school room when they heard a shrill whistle. Turning, they saw Sky Teacher standing on the back porch with a plate of scraps. He whistled again, then called, "You two haven't seen White Tail around this morning, have you?"

Justin suddenly realized that he hadn't seen the little dog since the day before. When they both shook their heads, Sky Teacher set the plate of scraps down on the back porch. "He's probably off chasing rabbits. Maybe he'll smell this sausage and come home."

Justin and Jenny stacked their suitcases and sleeping bags in a corner, then hurried out to help Sky Teacher set up chairs for the service. "The Cree are used to sitting in a circle—not on benches facing the front like the traditional 'white man' churches," Sky Teacher told them.

There was no piano or pulpit, either. They had just finished setting up the chairs when the first Indian children trooped into the church. The children stared at them with big dark eyes. Justin and Jenny stared back with equal interest.

A good-sized group of children had gathered by the time Sky Teacher began a lively chorus, but there were few adults—and most were elderly. Catching Sky Teacher's occasional glance at the door, Justin guessed that he'd expected a larger attendance.

Sky Teacher was just opening his Bible when boisterous shouts and a pounding of feet erupted outside the church. Then the uneven rhythm of the drums joined in. Male voices took up an Indian chant that rose to drown out Sky Teacher's calm tones. The Indian missionary raised his voice, but the disturbance outside grew louder, and at last he had to give up. Shutting his Bible, he closed the meeting with a prayer.

The Parkers and Sky Teacher filed out after the rest of the small congregation. A white pickup was parked across the gravel road. Just outside the church, a circle of Philip Dumont's followers swayed and pounded their feet against the ground to the beat of several Indian drums. Philip Dumont stood near the drums, his arms folded across his leather tunic, as he watched the dancers. A growing crowd was gathering around Dumont.

The Sunday school children ran eagerly down the steps to join the crowd, but Justin and Jenny stopped beside their parents and Sky Teacher at the top of the church steps. Justin searched the crowd for Yellow Dog's shaved head. He saw no sign of Philip Dumont's assistant, but he did notice Bear Paw in the circle of dancers.

"How can those guys come here and wreck your service?" Justin demanded hotly. "I mean, you weren't doing anything to hurt them!"

"Yeah, what a bunch of creeps!" added Jenny.

"The Indian activists aren't all bad, kids!" began Sky Teacher. "You see, for many years the U.S. government tried to stamp out Indian culture. I remember being punished for speaking my own Cree language at the government boarding school we all had to attend. We were taught to be ashamed of anything that was part of our Indian past. It was activists like these who fought to keep the Indian arts and music and culture alive. They haven't always gone about it in the best way, but—" He broke off when a news van roared up to the church. A news woman jumped out, with cameramen trailing.

"Hey, it's that reporter!" Justin exclaimed.

"Mr. Dumont said he'd have some 'proof' about Death Canyon today. I'll bet that's why she's here!" added Jenny.

"Well, come on! Let's find out!" The twins caught up to the reporter just as she thrust her microphone at Philip Dumont. "Wouldn't you call this interruption of a church service an invasion of these people's rights?" she demanded.

The drums and dancing instantly stopped. Unfolding his arms, Philip Dumont stepped forward and looked full into the TV camera. "We're doing nothing illegal here!" he said coldly.

"We are simply holding a powwow on reservation property. *This* is the traditional way of worship of the Indian people!"

The emphasis in his voice was clear as he glared at the small, wood-frame church. The reporter jumped on his statement. "Mr. Dumont, are you saying that other church groups have no right to practice their religion here on the reservation?"

"I'm saying we don't need the 'white man' forcing his religion on the Indian people. The spirits demand that we return to the ways of our ancestors!" Philip Dumont whirled suddenly on Justin and Jenny who were standing quietly behind the news crew.

"You two! You were attending Sky Teacher's church service. Would you call yourselves one of these . . . Christians?"

The TV reporter turned around. The cameraman immediately focused his video camera on the startled pair, and an expectant silence fell over the crowd. Justin gulped as he glanced around the circle of watching eyes, some curious, others hostile. He looked back to where his parents were standing with Sky Teacher on the church steps. Philip Dumont followed his glance.

"I asked *you,* kid!" he taunted. "Not your parents!"

Justin turned to meet the activist leader's mocking gaze. His heart was racing, but he spoke up clearly. "Yes, I *am* a Christian. I've asked Jesus to forgive my sins and be my Savior."

Jenny moved over until her shoulder touched her brother's. She lifted her small chin in the air. "So have I. I'm a Christian, too!"

A derisive smile played around Philip Dumont's thin lips. He turned back to the TV camera. "I've made my point! These children follow the Christian religion of their ancestors. The Indian people must follow the ways of their own ancestors."

Justin's mouth twisted in an ironic smile as Dumont ranted on. Justin jumped when the blonde reporter thrust the microphone in his face again. "Would you like to share the joke with the rest of us?"

He glanced nervously around the crowd, then faced the camera. "Well, I was just thinking about what my dad told me about *his* ancestors—the ones who gave him and me all this red hair! You see, they were Vikings. You know, the ones with those funny boats with the dragon heads. They weren't Christians at all!"

"They sure weren't!" Jenny added. "They worshiped Odin and Thor and a bunch of other gods. We read about it at school. They spent most of their time sailing around burning villages and chopping peoples' heads off!"

She took a breath, and Justin jumped in. "My dad said it wasn't until the first missionaries came along preaching about Jesus and loving your enemies that the Vikings finally settled down. Of course, they didn't all become Christians, but enough of them did so that they gave up those 'traditional ways' you were talking about and stopped killing people!"

Anger twisted Philip Dumont's features. But a smile rippled across the crowd, and the cameraman chuckled as he spoke. "You know, kid, those Viking ancestors of yours used to raid *my* ancestors every summer. Personally, I'm glad they ran into those missionaries." The reporter turned the microphone back toward Dumont and said purposefully, "This has been an interesting discussion, but it isn't why we're here today. Mr. Dumont, you promised us some proof of your claims that the Death Canyon area is a sacred burial ground of the Indian people."

The thunder of hoofbeats cut off any answer as a dozen horsemen galloped up to the crowd. At the head of the group rode Yellow Dog and Windy Boy, the elderly chairman of the tribal council.

"You'll have your proof." Philip Dumont made a mocking gesture toward several spare horses that Yellow Dog was leading. "That is, if you're up to some horseback riding!"

The reporter dropped her equipment into a small shoulder bag and, ignoring the consequences to her smart trouser suit, swung competently onto one of the spare horses.

Sky Teacher stepped forward as the cameraman climbed onto another. "Windy Boy, you don't mind if I tag along on this expedition, do you?"

Philip Dumont looked furious, but when the tribal chairman nodded, he shrugged his shoulders and swung into the saddle of the remaining horse. Sky Teacher strode rapidly toward the stable. Justin and Jenny turned pleading eyes on their parents. "Please, can't we go, too?"

Dad and Mom exchanged a thoughtful glance. "I really don't think your mom and I would be too welcome out there," Dad said slowly.

"But—we—oh, please!"

Dad held up his hand for silence. "Now just a minute! I didn't say you two couldn't go—*if* John doesn't mind. In fact, you just might learn something!"

"Tell John we'll have dinner waiting when you get back," Mom added.

Philip Dumont led the riding party single file down into a gully. This time Justin noted the entrance carefully. Jenny nudged him as they reached the shallow cave at the end of the ravine. It was empty. When they rode out onto the plateau, Philip Dumont led the way along the rock wall that circled it. He stopped in front of a low opening carved into the limestone.

The cameraman already had the video camera rolling as the tribal leaders dismounted. This cave looked much deeper than the one where Justin and Jenny had first seen the skeleton. From horseback they couldn't see anything but a black hole. Windy Boy stooped to crawl into the opening. Long moments passed before he stepped out and lifted up an ancient-looking stone peace pipe and an age-blackened rattle.

"Mr. Dumont has seen the vision truly!" he announced quietly. "This is indeed the burial place of an Indian warrior. The skeleton is of great age, and with it we found other items meant to cheer his way to the other world. There is no longer any doubt that Death Canyon was once a sacred burial ground of our people."

"We saw them put those things in there last night!" Jenny whispered.

"Yeah! Their 'sacred burial!'" Justin hissed. "They're not going to get away with this!"

But he was just kneeing the Appaloosa forward when Sky Teacher laid a firm hand on the horse's neck. "Let it go," he said quietly.

The tribal leaders mounted their horses, and the riding party trotted across the plateau toward an object on the ground. Justin and Jenny followed the group. Both of them gasped in horror as they recognized the dead animal on the plateau floor. It was White Tail, Sky Teacher's small dog!

Sky Teacher and Windy Boy examined the small form. After a long moment, Windy Boy stood. "There are no signs of snake bite or any other natural cause of death."

Philip Dumont raised his arms dramatically and shouted, "It is as I said! Sky Teacher has brought down the anger of the spirits. It is they who have brought death here today!" He turned his fiery glare on Sky Teacher. "Today the spirits that protect Death Canyon have destroyed a dog! Take care that you—and those under your care—are not next!"

Chapter Eight

ONE MILLION DOLLARS

Hostility burned across the faces of the tribal leaders as Philip Dumont finished his dramatic declaration. One middle-aged man, fear etched on his dark features, made a curious sign in the air as he stared at Sky Teacher, then at the dead dog.

"We have seen enough! We will leave here at once." Windy Boy turned to Sky Teacher. "I'm sorry about White Tail, Sky Teacher. I will take care of him. Why don't you take these two home."

"Just a minute!" the blonde TV reporter interrupted. "We haven't finished filming the burial site. And we'd like to bring out an archeologist later today to dig up that cave. This is really big news!"

"You have your news!" Windy Boy answered shortly. "This is our land. We do not 'dig up' the burial sites of our ancestors! As a sacred burial ground of the Cree people, this area is now off-limits to any nontribal member."

"I doubt you'll talk many tribal members into coming up here, either." murmured one of the tribal leaders.

Disgruntled, the reporter and her cameraman climbed back onto their horses. Justin gritted his teeth at the smug satisfaction on Philip Dumont's face. Swinging onto Dark Cloud's back, Sky Teacher motioned to them. Reluctantly Justin kicked the Appaloosa into a trot and followed Sky Teacher back across the plateau.

Conversation was impossible as they rode single file through the ravine. But as soon as they came out into the open, Jenny burst out, "That was no sacred burial cave they found!"

"Yeah!" Justin added indignantly. "We *saw* Mr. Dumont and Yellow Dog put those things there last night—and the skeleton!"

Sky Teacher didn't answer. Instead he pulled a small, rusted object out of a pocket and passed it over to Justin. "Do you know what this is, Justin?"

Justin turned the small, round object over. He shrugged and passed it on to Jenny. "It looks like an old metal button."

"That's exactly what it is, kids." Sky Teacher held out his hand for the piece of metal. "It's the button off a U.S. Cavalry uniform from more than a hundred years ago. I found it lodged in that skeleton Philip Dumont dug up out of Death Canyon!"

Justin sat up straight in the saddle. "You mean—"

"That's right. The man out there in that burial cave wasn't even Indian! Now a fanatic Indian activist might go to any extreme—including killing my dog—to protect a real historical burial ground of our people. But we at least know that Philip Dumont's burial cave is a fake."

"Then why didn't you let us tell them?" Jenny demanded. "Now your tribe is going to believe Mr. Dumont's lies about the spirits and all!"

Sky Teacher shook his head. "Kids, Philip Dumont has been after two things since the moment he set foot on this reservation.

One, to stop any exploration of the Death Canyon land and have it declared a historical site. Two, to turn the tribe against me and my preaching of the gospel. He'd love to have me and the mission run off the reservation.

"Now *I* believe what you saw out there last night, but you have no proof! It would be your word against Philip Dumont *and* the tribal council. People here on the reservation know I've been fighting for mineral development on that land. Philip Dumont would convince the tribal council that I put you two up to this. It would just make the situation that much worse."

"So what are you going to do?" Justin asked.

"Nothing—*yet*." Sky Teacher tossed the rusted button up and down in his hand. "I want to know why Philip Dumont would perpetrate a fraud he must know will be uncovered sooner or later. I think we'll just wait and see what he does next."

He gave Justin and Jenny a keen look. "And I would appreciate it if you two would just keep quiet about this for now."

Justin suddenly remembered the faint yelp he'd heard from the church window the night before. "Mr. Dumont and Yellow Dog! I'll bet *they* took White Tail out there! That's what they were doing outside the parsonage last night!"

"That burlap bag!" Jenny looked sick. "I'll bet they had him in there all the time! They probably chloroformed him or something so no one would hear."

Sky Teacher sighed heavily. "I figured Dumont's hand was in there somewhere. But I doubt an autopsy would show any cause of death. Philip Dumont is a clever man."

That evening, Sky Teacher pulled an old portable TV out of a closet and hooked it up to watch the news. Justin and Jenny were fascinated to see the whole story of Death Canyon played out on the small screen, including their own exchange with Philip Dumont.

"I didn't get a chance to tell you," Dad said, as the picture moved from the twins back to Dumont, "that I was really proud of the way you stood up for your faith out there."

As the news clip came to an end, the blonde reporter looked out at her TV audience and asked, "Will this discovery put an end to the Big Sky Indian Reservation's plans for mineral development? Perhaps the question is, were there ever any mineral resources to be developed?"

"Maybe she's right!" Sky Teacher turned off the TV. "They haven't found any mineral wealth on the reservation so far. Why should we think this new land would be any different?"

The next two days were quiet on the reservation. *It's too quiet,* Justin thought uneasily. *Like the calm before a storm.* There was no sight of the NARC activists or the news van. The twins took a ride on horseback, and Justin worked with Dad to get the SUV running again. On Tuesday, Sky Teacher drove the Parkers out to his favorite trout stream.

It was Wednesday as they were finishing supper that the phone rang. Sky Teacher left the table to answer it. When he returned, he said abruptly, "The tribal council has called an emergency town meeting for this evening. I wasn't even notified. In fact, I wouldn't have found out until it was over if one of the church members hadn't called."

Mom caught his glance around at the remains of the meal. "Don't worry about the kitchen," she said quickly. "The twins and I'll take care of it. Why don't you and Ron head on over."

Justin and Jenny exchanged a wry glance, but Sky Teacher looked so troubled they didn't even attempt a protest. They cleaned and washed hastily until Mom said with a smile, "Go on. I can finish. I can see you're only half here anyway."

Justin and Jenny took off at a run down the dusty road that led to the Community Center. As they burst breathlessly into the lobby, they heard Sky Teacher's deep voice from a loudspeaker overhead. "Brothers, we have heard much about the past in these last weeks. Old hatreds have been stirred up—old wounds!"

Slipping into the back of the auditorium, Justin and Jenny spotted Sky Teacher standing at the microphone on the platform up front. Behind him was a long table at which sat a row of Cree men and women. One was the elderly tribal leader the twins had already met, Robert Windy Boy. He was holding a gavel. This must be the tribal council.

"No one here will deny that we have lost the greatness, the vast lands we once held. It's nothing unique to our people. One nation has been kicking another off their land since the dawn of human history. Our own people claimed their land by driving out earlier tribes. We ourselves came to this area because a stronger tribe drove us from our ancestral lands."

A respectful silence reigned as Sky Teacher's deep voice rose to the back of the auditorium. *Way to go, Sky Teacher!* Justin silently cheered as he glanced around at the attentive faces of the other tribal members.

"There isn't one of us who wouldn't love to see our people

ruling the western plains as they once did. But times and nations change. The old world is gone, much as we regret it. Anger and bitterness will not change that. We must not look to the past, but to the future—and the present! We must work to build a better future for our people in *this* world, the world in which we now live. And that means working and living together in peace—Indian and non-Indian!"

Thunderous applause swept across the auditorium as Sky Teacher stepped back from the microphone. The tribal council nodded approval. Then Philip Dumont stepped up to the podium. To Justin's surprise, he was smiling!

"Sky Teacher, you are absolutely right!" The activist leader had lost the dramatic tones of his outdoor speeches. He spoke in the clipped tones of a businessman as he turned to the audience. "In fact, it is because of my own concern for the future as well as the past of the Indian people that this meeting has been called tonight. I have presented a proposal to the Big Sky tribal council—a proposal they have graciously allowed me to share with you."

He paused as an excited murmur swept across the auditorium. The activist leader waited until it died away before he announced, "On behalf of the Indian Historical Foundation, I am prepared to offer the Big Sky Indian Reservation the sum of *one million dollars* for the ten thousand acres of undeveloped land adjoining this reservation."

The auditorium erupted in a babble of excited voices. Windy Boy pounded his gavel on the table to restore order. Then a man stood to his feet. He was holding a toddler in his arms. The tribal chairman nodded for him to speak.

"Excuse me, but I seem to remember that we put a lot of effort and tribal money into getting that land for the reservation. Mr. Dumont's offer sounds great, but with more than three thousand members on the tribal rolls, that only works out to about three hundred dollars per person. How is selling our land to Mr. Dumont going to help the tribe?"

Windy Boy nodded to Philip Dumont. The activist leader answered smoothly. "That's the best part of this sale, friends. If you turn this land over to the Indian Historical Foundation, all of the land, *and* the sacred burial grounds, will remain in trust for the Indian people. To coin a phrase, you're not losing the land, you're gaining a million dollars! May I remind you that this is twice what you paid for it?"

Sky Teacher had stepped back to one side of the podium. But the microphone picked up his comment. "If there are minerals on that land, a million dollars is only a fraction of what it's worth!"

Philip Dumont turned savagely on Sky Teacher. But he forced a smile as he glanced out over the audience. "There *are* no minerals on that land, Sky Teacher. And we have a geologist here tonight whose survey will bear that out. Mr. Siedman?"

A man in a business suit rose from the front row. He was short and thin with prematurely white hair.

Sky Teacher said sharply, "I wasn't aware that the tribal council was conducting any mineral exploration!"

"We don't have to keep *you* informed of the decisions of the tribal council!" a council member answered just as sharply, his dark face hostile. It was the same middle-aged man who had made the sign in the air against evil when he'd seen White Tail's lifeless body.

Windy Boy raised his hand for silence. He turned to Sky Teacher. "I know we agreed that you would find us an exploration team. But Mr. Siedman here has offered his services to the tribe. His development company did a survey of their own on that land not long before we bought it. He has offered to share the results of that survey at no cost to the tribe. Unfortunately, the survey is very clear. There are no minerals."

The tribal chairman frowned. "We should have known of this survey before we ever signed that contract last year. But, thanks to Mr. Dumont, we now have a chance to recover the tribe's investment."

Philip Dumont leaned forward to speak into the microphone. "Mr. Sky Teacher here has been lobbying for funds for job opportunities and scholarships. I've given the tribe an answer to that need, and all he can do is come up with one objection after another!"

He looked Sky Teacher up and down contemptuously. "How much do you *really* care about the future of this tribe?"

Sky Teacher ignored the sarcastic question. Stepping up to the podium, he said gravely, "If the survey results really show that there are no minerals on our land, then Mr. Dumont's offer is very generous. I withdraw my objections."

Philip Dumont turned impatiently to the tribal council. "You called this meeting to vote on my proposal. I can't stay much longer in this area, and the money for this project won't be available for long. I must have an answer to my proposal soon!"

A babble of voices broke out, but Sky Teacher didn't take any further part in the debate. He slipped into the back row beside Justin and Jenny as Windy Boy pounded his gavel and called for a secret ballot. Justin studied Sky Teacher out of the corner of his eye as each tribal member placed their vote into the ballot box. If he was worried about the outcome of the vote, he sure didn't show it.

The whole auditorium quieted to an expectant hush as the tribal council counted the ballots. One of the tribal leaders handed Windy Boy a piece of paper. The tribal chairman rose to his feet.

"The vote is 315 in favor of this sale and 16 against," he announced gravely. "The land in question will therefore be sold to the Indian Historical Foundation for the sum of one million dollars!"

Chapter Nine

EXPLOSIVE DANGER

Philip Dumont stepped up to the microphone. "Thank you! My lawyer will prepare the contract of sale immediately. Your money will be deposited in the tribal accounts by the end of the week."

"It is we who thank you, Mr. Dumont." Windy Boy looked across to the back of the auditorium. "And I know we can count on Sky Teacher's legal services to review the contract when it is ready."

Sky Teacher rose to his feet. Justin almost laughed to see the smug look wiped off Philip Dumont's face as the missionary nodded his assent. But Justin wasn't laughing as he, Dad, and Jenny walked with Sky Teacher back to the parsonage. He couldn't help feeling annoyed as he glanced up at the tall missionary. Sky Teacher didn't seem at all upset at the outcome of the vote.

"Don't you mind about the vote?" he demanded suddenly. "I mean, you've lost the land. Uncle Pete won't be able to come and look for minerals. Don't you care?"

Sky Teacher smiled down at Justin's scowling, freckled face. "Justin, I told you I needed to know what Philip Dumont wanted out of all this. Well, now I know! The activists—the speeches—everything he's done has been for the single purpose of getting his hands on that land. And since we at least know his sacred burial grounds are a fake, the only question is why he wants that land so badly!"

Justin shook his head, bewildered. "But—he already knows there aren't any minerals or anything on that land! What *could* he want it for?"

"I don't know. But I think I'll make a few phone calls and see what I can find out."

The next morning the Parkers drove into Great Falls, the nearest city to Big Sky Indian Reservation. With a population of more than fifty-five thousand, Great Falls was the major shopping center for the wide-open spaces of eastern Montana. Mom and Dad stopped to browse through a secondhand bookstore. Justin and Jenny strolled down the street, pausing every few minutes to admire the Western goods in the store windows.

"Hey!" Justin stopped abruptly. Grabbing Jenny's arm, he yanked her into the shadow of the shop doorway.

"What—?" Jenny bit off her angry protest when she caught sight of the two men who were coming out of an office building just beyond a saloon. One was the short, thin geologist they had seen the night before. The other—looking more like a business executive than an Indian activist in a neat, well-fitting gray suit—was Philip Dumont!

"Well, well! Look who's running around in a business suit! And after the way he's always telling the reservation people to go back to the 'ways of their ancestors!'" Justin gave the two men a speculative look. They were standing, heads close together in the shadow of a wide, glass doorway. "I wonder what *he's* up to, sneaking around here talking to Mr. Siedman!"

"What do you mean, sneaking around? Why shouldn't he be here? I mean, he doesn't live on the reservation. Maybe this is where he keeps his office!" Jenny broke off as Dumont stepped out of the doorway. Mr. Siedman disappeared back into the office building. Philip Dumont glanced up and down the street, then ducked around the corner.

"See!" Justin said triumphantly. "He doesn't want anyone to see him. I told you he was sneaking around!"

Jenny didn't answer, but she made no protest when Justin insisted on inspecting the building into which Mr. Siedman had disappeared. Justin peered through the wide glass doors, but he saw no sign of the geologist. He stopped to study a bronzed metal directory on the wall beside the door.

"Let's see! Charles Bowman—Pediatrician, Roger Pederson—Dental Surgeon, Dugan and Dugan Accounting, Universal Corporation, Sterling Jewelers—"

"Is there supposed to be a clue on there?" Jenny demanded tartly, reading over his shoulder.

"Justin! Jenny!" It was Mom. They hurried back up the street as Dad added an impatient honk from their parked car.

It was still early in the afternoon when they got back to the reservation. One of Mom's cousins was holding a family reunion the next day in Billings, a city almost eight hours away. Mom and Dad had decided to go and were planning to drive late into the night to get there in time. The reservation had been quiet since the tribal meeting, so they had agreed to let Justin and Jenny stay with Sky Teacher.

"We'll be back Saturday. Are you sure you two will be okay?" Mom asked as Dad tossed their suitcase into the station wagon. "We've left the number where we'll be staying in case there's a problem."

"Don't worry, Mom," Justin grinned. "I'll keep Jenny out of trouble."

Jenny elbowed him sharply in the ribs. "You mean, I'll keep *you* out of trouble."

After supper that evening, Sky Teacher dug out a dusty box of Rummikub tiles. But he seemed preoccupied, and Justin and Jenny excused themselves early to walk back over to the church.

The Sunday school room where they slept was stifling after the heat of the day. Justin threw open the window, but the air outside was only slightly cooler. He leaned his elbows on the windowsill. "I'd sure like to know what Mr. Siedman was doing this morning with Philip Dumont—he and his fancy suits."

"Why shouldn't he talk to him?" Jenny said reasonably. "I mean, if Mr. Dumont is buying that land, maybe he just wanted to see that survey they were talking about."

"Yeah, and maybe *he* was the one who recommended Mr. Siedman to the tribe! Maybe Mr. Siedman's lying about the survey just like Mr. Dumont lied about the burial ground. If we just knew what they were talking about . . ."

He sighed as Jenny raised skeptical eyebrows and continued, "Yeah, I guess it's wishful thinking. It's just—well, I've been praying that Sky Teacher would win out—about the minerals and all. And now look what's happened! That phony's got the land, and the tribe still thinks the spirits are angry at Sky Teacher."

"I know. I've been praying things would work out so Sky Teacher could invite Marie here—maybe even get married. He's such a nice guy. He deserves to be happy." Jenny gave a sudden shudder. "But one thing's for sure. White Tail wasn't phony. I mean, what could kill him without leaving a mark? Sky Teacher said himself he wasn't poisoned or anything. And that ghost— or whatever it was—we saw it ourselves! It was real!"

Finally a night breeze began to cool the room, and they stretched out on top of their sleeping bags.

It was the heat that woke him. Or was it a noise? The room was even hotter than when he'd gone to bed. Justin wiped a damp hand across his sweaty face. He stopped as he caught the phosphorescent glow of his wristwatch. Three A.M. He'd better get back to sleep. Then, through the open door that led to the church sanctuary, he heard a noise—a soft scraping and a long, hardly audible hiss. He rolled over and sat up, but the motion left him dizzy and nauseated, and a headache pounded at his temples. If he could just get a breath of fresh air! He stood and groped his way toward the window. It was jammed shut! Hadn't they left it open? He shook his head. Something was very wrong! He stumbled across the room and tripped over Jenny, but she didn't make a sound. He grabbed her and shook her furiously, but she didn't stir.

"Jenny, wake up!" Fear mixed with the dizziness that clouded his mind. Justin staggered toward where he knew the open door must be. At last his fingers brushed against the doorjamb. He fumbled for the light switch.

The sudden brightness hurt his unfocused eyes. He squinted blearily. Was that a human-shaped shadow out there in the hallway? The shadow blurred into a dark fog. His fingers slid from the doorjamb, and he slumped to the floor. From somewhere down a long, black tunnel an angry voice insisted, "There's kids in there! There weren't supposed to be kids in there!"

A cool breeze played over Justin's face as he opened his eyes. He stared at two hazy, yellow blobs that bobbed overhead. They made him dizzy, so he squeezed his eyes shut. When he opened them again, the yellow blobs became one full moon. He was lying flat under a star-strewn sky. Something sharp was prodding the small of his back.

Justin sat up. Pulling a long, sharp twig out of his shirt, he looked around. He was sitting on his sleeping bag in the middle of the overgrown lot that stretched between the church and the tribal stable. *How did I get here?* His blurred gaze fell on his sister stretched out beside him on her own sleeping bag. Justin dropped his aching head into his hands. *Why are we sleeping outside?*

Jenny groaned. Rolling over, she clutched at her temples. "Oh, my head! What happened?"

Justin shook his head without lifting it from his hands. "I don't know. We . . . we were in the church. Then I woke up . . . I think!" A faint recollection came back. "I heard voices . . . or was that a dream?"

Jenny struggled to a sitting position. Her puzzled gaze fell on a large, rectangular object that glinted in the moonlight. "Our suitcase! What's it doing out here!"

But Justin didn't get a chance to answer. A thunderous noise burst across the night, throwing them both face down to the ground. They huddled unmoving as a shower of small objects rained down on their unprotected backs.

It was over within seconds. As the thunder died, a light blinked on in the parsonage. Shouts and the shrill barking of dogs broke out from the houses just down the road. But Justin and Jenny didn't even notice. Huddled close together, they stared across the field with wide-eyed horror. Where the little, white church had been just moments before now lay a mound of jagged lumber and debris!

Chapter Ten

INDIAN DAYS

"Justin! Jenny!" Sky Teacher's deep tones slowly penetrated their ringing ears. They staggered to their feet. Justin waved frantically as he caught sight of the Indian missionary standing beside the heap of rubble that had once been a church. "We're over here!"

Sky Teacher raced across the field. His grim expression lightened as he looked over the dirt-splattered twins. "Are you both in one piece?"

"I . . . I think so!" Jenny shook the debris from her hair and clothes. "But I'm not sure how we got out here!"

Sky Teacher's sharp eyes took in the suitcase and sleeping bags scattered on the ground. "It looks like you were sleeping out here—not a bad idea in this heat! Are you telling me you don't remember?"

Jenny glanced doubtfully at Justin. "I'm sure we were in the church when I fell asleep! But that's all I remember until I woke up just before the explosion."

Justin shook his head. His headache was fading as he breathed deeply of the cool night air, but he was no longer sure of anything. He still retained a vague impression of heat and angry voices, but his memory was cloudy. Maybe they *had* carried their stuff out to get away from the heat! The tribal police chief showed up some time later. He listened with a fatherly smile to Justin's stumbling account of the night.

"You say you couldn't breathe—then you think you heard voices—then you woke up out here on your sleeping bag."

He patted Justin on the back. "It sounds to me like you were having a bad dream. Just be thankful you *were* sleeping out here!" He gestured toward the heap of shattered timber. "No one could have lived through that!"

They waited until daylight before they called their parents. Dad answered the phone. "We're coming back just as soon as we can get away! The family reunion isn't that important. But the car overheated again, and we're going to have to take it to a mechanic. It'll probably be late by the time we get in."

The tribal police chief walked into the kitchen just as Justin hung up the phone. He shook his head. "This explosion doesn't make sense, Sky Teacher. There's no sign of arson or sabotage— or even a fire. If it was a bomb or dynamite, we'd find localized signs showing where the explosion actually went off. But it looks to me like the whole place blew at once—so fast there was no time for a fire to start! I saw something like this once before in Great Falls. If I didn't know better, I'd almost think a leak pumped that place full of gas, then a spark set the whole place to blow at once. But since there's not a natural gas hook-up around here . . ."

"Wouldn't we have smelled natural gas?" Justin cut in, still trying hard to remember what had happened last night. "My grandpa's camper has it, and it smells pretty awful."

"That's right. Natural gas has a pretty strong odor, and there certainly wasn't a trace of it around." The police chief shrugged. "Well, the cause of this explosion may just remain a mystery."

He glanced at Sky Teacher. "You know what people will say."

Sky Teacher looked grim. "I imagine they're already saying that Philip Dumont was right. The spirits destroyed the church like they destroyed my dog."

They walked the police chief back to his car and watched as the now-familiar white pickup roared up to the parsonage. Philip Dumont stepped out and walked toward them. He wore Indian dress again, but he carried a briefcase.

"I'm sorry to hear about your trouble last night, Sky Teacher." He paused to stare with an expressionless face at the blackened heap across the yard. *Yeah, you look real sorry,* Justin thought.

Sky Teacher made no comment. Arms folded across his chest, he watched Dumont with narrowed eyes. Philip Dumont glanced with distaste at the children and other curious spectators who had gathered at the explosion site. "Could we step inside, Sky Teacher? I have a proposition for you."

"I don't see why not." Sky Teacher courteously waved him toward the house. Justin and Jenny slipped into a far corner of the living room.

Without waiting for an invitation, Philip Dumont sat down and opened his briefcase. "I've done some checking on you, Sky Teacher. You've got quite a record—service in the Marines, scholarships to Berkeley, your own law practice. A real credit to the Indian people!"

"You didn't come here to pass out compliments, Dumont." Sky Teacher spoke dryly. "What do you want?"

"It's simple!" Philip Dumont's answer didn't match the

coldness of his eyes. "We've had our differences, but I respect your desire to help your people. I've checked on your property deeds here. This place isn't reservation land. It belongs to the Indian Bible Mission. If you will sell me this land, I will donate it to the tribe for a cultural center and donate the funds to build it."

Justin and Jenny exchanged an astonished glance, but Sky Teacher just asked mildly. "So what am I—and the church—supposed to do?"

Philip Dumont shrugged. "You'll find that I'm generous enough to permit you to rebuild elsewhere. Right now you have nothing. Your church building is gone, and I think the hostility you've encountered must have convinced you that there isn't much point in remaining here on the reservation."

"Hostility *you've* stirred up!" Sky Teacher interjected.

Philip Dumont's pleasant expression slipped for a moment, but he forced a smile. "Sky Teacher, you must face the fact that the Indian people don't want you—or your 'white man's' religion. Build yourself a nice church somewhere else. Or go back to that well-paying law practice in California. I can't imagine why you gave it up to come here anyway."

He glanced distastefully around the shabby living room. Sky Teacher leaned forward. "Maybe you're right, Dumont. Maybe my people *don't* want me here. But they need me—*and* the knowledge of the one true God!"

Sky Teacher stood up and walked to the door. "You might as well give up, Dumont. None of your little tricks will succeed in getting me off this reservation."

The other man's pretense of friendliness evaporated as he

slammed the briefcase shut and strode out the screen door, which Sky Teacher held open. "I trust you'll live to regret this decision, Sky Teacher!"

Justin gave a long, low whistle of approval as the door slammed behind Dumont. "You were great, Sky Teacher! I'm glad you turned that creep down!" Jenny's face clouded over. "But what'll you do now? Your church is gone!"

"It doesn't take a church building to worship God, Jenny!" He grinned as he looked from one twin to the other. "Hey kids, have you forgotten what today is? There's a parade starting in an hour! Why don't you stop worrying about my affairs and enjoy your first taste of Indian Days."

Sky Teacher disappeared into the bedroom. When he joined them a few minutes later, he was wearing the chieftain's outfit again. "I've got to go on ahead. I'll meet you two at the fair grounds after the parade."

An enormous crowd of spectators had lined Main Street by the time Justin and Jenny arrived. They found a place just as the drums signaled the beginning of the parade. An Indian warrior bearing the American flag rode at the head of the parade, his white-and-black pony sidestepping daintily.

"Hey, that's Windy Boy!" Justin shouted above the roar of the crowd as he recognized the solemn face framed in white and red feathers. He waved wildly. The elderly Indian leader kept his gaze fixed straight ahead, but a faint smile showed that he had seen them.

Floats and other horsemen came behind the tribal chairman. A boy about their age rode on top of a fringed and feathered float. The bright beadwork on his head, arm bands, and buck skin tunic added color to the tanned leather. He held out what looked like a shepherd's staff wrapped in fur and fringed with long, white feathers.

The last float was passing, and the twins still hadn't seen any sign of Sky Teacher.

"There he is!" Jenny suddenly nudged her brother. A whole party of Indian warriors was trotting down the street, their sharp spears raised high. Justin picked out Dark Cloud prancing in the center, but he hardly recognized Sky Teacher in the war paint that now masked his bronzed features. Sky Teacher smiled and waved his spear as the party swept by.

The war party marked the end of the parade. The crowd began to break up and drift toward the fairgrounds. Jenny let out a contented sigh. "That was wonderful."

Justin tugged at her. "Come on! Sky Teacher'll be waiting."

For most of the year, the fairgrounds were just a grassy field dotted with somewhat dilapidated wooden structures. But today they were bright with banners and Indian flags. Dozens of canvas or deerskin tepees circled the outskirts of the field—some a plain creamy white, others decorated with colorful geometric figures or animal designs. The rows of campers and parked vehicles added a twenty-first century touch. Behind a wall of unpainted boards was the rodeo arena.

They threaded their way through the crowds. Tribal members in Indian costumes mixed casually with local cowboys and tourists in shorts with clicking cameras.

"Hi, Justin! Hi, Jenny!" A small girl in a long, blue tunic and high moccasin boots dashed by. Justin had to look hard to remember he'd met her in Sunday school just a few days before.

There were none of the carnival rides Justin and Jenny associated with county fairs. But there were plenty of food stands and Indian craft displays. Long tables under a roofed shelter were piled high with striped blankets as well as beadwork and handcrafted jewelry. Jenny stopped to drool over a selection of turquoise-and-silver bracelets.

Justin picked up a pair of moccasins beaded in a starburst pattern. He glanced around. There was no one at the table, but a group of Indian women was gossiping over an intricately beaded leather shirt three tables away. "I wonder if those ladies would know how much these cost?"

"They're not for sale."

"Sky Teacher!" Justin and Jenny spun around, and Justin dropped the moccasins back on the table. Sky Teacher had removed his feathered headdress and washed off the war paint, but he still wore his leather leggings and tunic. He nodded toward the brilliantly colored blankets and leather goods.

"These things aren't for sale. They're for a potlatch later on today."

"A potlatch?" Jenny repeated. "What's *that?*"

"It's a traditional custom of the Indian people." Sky Teacher nodded toward the group of women still visiting three tables down. "Those ladies have probably been working all year to make these things. Today and during the rest of Indian Days, they'll give them away to friends and relatives to show their appreciation and respect."

He waved a fringed arm down the row of tables. "But don't worry. There are a few stands along here that sell crafts to the tourists."

He led them to a stall that sold beadwork, Indian jewelry, and other souvenirs. Justin sorted through the moccasins while Jenny picked out some postcards to send to friends back home. Justin was counting out his money when the drums started. A slow, mournful chant rose above the bustle of the crowd.

"It sounds like they're starting the dancing," said Sky Teacher. "Come on, you'll enjoy this!" He led them through the food and craft stands to the dance enclosure that stood in the center of the fairgrounds. This was a large, round structure with wooden posts for walls, a high roof, and clipped grass for a floor. Spectators and families relaxed on blankets and chairs around the edge, but a dozen men were gathered to one side around the biggest drum they had ever seen. In the center, people of all ages had joined hands in a large circle.

Sky Teacher and the twins stopped just inside the enclosure to watch the dancers—some in Indian dress, others in shorts or jeans—pound their feet enthusiastically to the rhythm of the drums. Justin suddenly frowned. *Hey, those dancers aren't—*

Jenny took the words out of his mind. "Hey, Sky Teacher, half those guys have brown and blonde hair! They're not tribal members, are they?"

Sky Teacher grinned. "As much as you are, Jenny! A lot of these people are more European than Indian in background, but they come to Indian Days to celebrate that part of their heritage. In the past, you see, you only needed as little as an eighth or sixteenth Indian blood to be on the tribal rolls. Even today you only need one Indian grandparent to be a tribal member. So a man can be more European than Indian and still be listed on a tribal roll."

"Like Philip Dumont!"

Sky Teacher gave Justin a sharp look. "What do you mean?"

Justin lifted his shoulders. "Well, *he* sure doesn't look Indian! But if he's an Indian activist, he's got to belong to some tribe, right?"

"I guess so!" Sky Teacher looked thoughtful. "You know, it might be interesting to know just what tribe he *does* belong to."

He glanced at his watch. "Well, I've got to get my gear ready for the rodeo. Why don't you two look around."

Justin and Jenny watched the dancing for a few minutes, then wandered off through the crowds. They squeezed back as a party of horsemen trotted past. Justin looked over the horses. None was as fine as Dark Cloud.

A sudden shove spun him around! A rider was pushing past the other horses so closely that his horse's shoulder had almost knocked Justin over. "Hey, watch it!" Justin took a hasty step back just as the horse's hind hoof came down where his foot had been. His own heavy shoe landed hard on Jenny's foot.

"Ouch!" Jenny yanked her foot away. Caught off balance, they both stumbled backward. Justin heard a grunt as they fell against something solid. Picking himself up, he saw that they had bumped into a small man whose neat business suit looked completely out of place in this holiday crowd. The man's briefcase was lying open on the ground, and he was down on his knees scrambling for the papers that had spilled.

"Oh, I'm so sorry!" Jenny exclaimed. She grabbed for the papers that the wind was beginning to scatter. Stammering out his own apology, Justin dropped down to help her. It wasn't until he turned to hand over the papers he had collected that he recognized the short, thin man with white hair.

"Hey, aren't you—" But before he could finish, Mr. Siedman grabbed the rescued papers from their hands and stuffed them into his briefcase. Snapping his briefcase shut, he melted into the crowd without a word of thanks.

Jenny bent over and picked up a sheet of paper. "Hey, look! Isn't this one of Mr. Siedman's? We'd better give it back!" She searched the crowd. "There he is."

The geologist was making his way toward a cluster of tepees on the far side of the craft stands. Dodging through the crowds, Justin and Jenny rounded the last stand just in time to see Mr. Siedman duck inside a canvas tepee.

They hurried toward the tepee, but they stopped short at the sound of a familiar angry voice coming from inside. Justin's eyebrows rose in astonishment. *What is Philip Dumont doing here with Mr. Siedman?*

"You shouldn't have come here!" Dumont exclaimed. "If the tribal elders see us together, they're going to start asking some awkward questions!"

"I wouldn't *have* to be here, Dumont, if you'd obey orders and keep in contact!" Mr. Siedman's low, clipped voice answered sharply. "Sky Teacher's been making phone calls. And if he finds out what we're *really* up to in Death Canyon, we're all in big trouble!"

Chapter Eleven

A SECRET MEETING

Justin beckoned frantically to his sister. "Did you hear that?"

Jenny nodded, her brown eyes wide as the significance of the two men's words sank in. "You were right! Mr. Siedman *is* working with Philip Dumont."

"Yeah, and it sounds like Siedman is the real boss!"

Justin broke off as he heard approaching footsteps and boisterous voices. A pair of tourists, cameras clicking, burst through the center of the dance lodge and started in their direction. Justin gave a silent jerk of the head, and they ducked around the back of the tepee. The men's low angry tones floated through the thin canvas walls.

"What do you mean, 'phone calls'?" Philip Dumont demanded.

"I mean just that!" Mr. Siedman snapped. "He's been digging up information about you—and me! Sky Teacher seems to have some friends in high places."

"Well, so do we!" Philip Dumont sounded peevish. "Besides, what does it matter? The tribe has already consented to the sale. They're signing the contract tonight. It's too late for Sky Teacher to do anything about it."

"Sky Teacher is a lawyer, remember?" Mr. Siedman shot back. "He's the only man on this reservation with the know-how to figure out what's going on. And he can get that contract turned upside down if he can prove fraud on your part."

"Well, I've done everything I can to get him off the reservation." Philip Dumont said defensively. "He just won't budge!"

"I told you, boss," a new voice joined in. "We should have blown up more than just that church!" Justin and Jenny both stiffened as they recognized Yellow Dog's surly tones.

Mr. Siedman's voice rose sharply. "I don't want to know what you two have been up to. Just take care of the problem!"

Footsteps crossed the floor of the tepee. Inching forward to peer around the side, Justin saw Mr. Siedman stride away toward the parking area. He rose to follow, but Jenny's warning tug reminded him that Philip Dumont and Yellow Dog could be coming out at any moment. Reluctantly, he crouched down to wait.

But the other two men showed no signs of leaving. Justin strained his ears, but he could make out only a faint murmur of voices inside the tepee. It seemed a long time before he heard footsteps move toward the entrance. There was a rustle of the door flap being lifted. Then Yellow Dog growled with satisfaction. "That'll take care of Sky Teacher all right—permanently!"

Philip Dumont's unpleasant chuckle floated back. "And if it doesn't, we can always leave him to the spirit of Chief Thunderbird!"

Justin and Jenny stared at each other in horror. As the sound of footsteps died away, Jenny jumped to her feet. "They're going to do something awful to Sky Teacher! We've got to warn him!"

Justin pulled her back down. "Just a minute! We don't want them to see us."

He peered cautiously around the side of the tepee. Philip Dumont and Yellow Dog were heading back toward the fair buildings. Both men were wearing the same ceremonial Indian dress they used for their rallies. Justin waited until the two men had rounded the dance lodge before he jumped up. "They're gone. Let's go find Sky Teacher!"

They began to run. Justin kept an eye out for Philip Dumont and Yellow Dog, but saw no sign of the two men. "Did you hear what Yellow Dog said?" he puffed. "They're the ones who blew up the church! But how?"

"Who knows!" Jenny panted. "What I want to know is what they meant about the spirit of Chief Thunderbird."

"Jenny, you *know* there aren't any ghosts!" Justin slowed to a walk as they reached the main fairgrounds. "At least this means Sky Teacher was right. Something really important's going on out there at Death Canyon. I wonder what Sky Teacher's phone calls were about."

Jenny stopped to stamp her foot. "What difference does it make? They said they're going to do something awful to him! We've got to get to him before they do!"

"I know, Jenny, but we've got to find him first." Justin glanced around the fairgrounds. *Where is everybody?* The crowds had dwindled to a few food stand attendants lazily switching flies from uneaten hot dogs and popcorn. Even the dance enclosure was empty.

A man's voice boomed from a nearby loudspeaker. A wild cheer rose from somewhere beyond the dance enclosure. Justin snapped his fingers. "Of course! Sky Teacher's riding in the rodeo. He'll be with the other riders."

They cut through the empty dance area to the rodeo arena on the other side. Cheers and shouts echoed from inside, but they hurried along the outside wall until they reached the maze of pens and corrals at the far end. Pushing open a long, low gate, Justin and Jenny slipped inside and fastened it behind them.

A sudden bellow startled them, and they jumped back against the gate. They gasped as a huge black bull thrust its head over the wooden railing to glare at them with small, red eyes. His horns were viciously sharp.

They quietly inched past the bull. The air was thick with dust kicked up by hurrying men and restless hooves. Jenny wiped a streak of dirt across her hot face. "I sure don't see him! Do you?"

Just ahead, four men wrestled a white-and-brown Appaloosa. The horse twisted and lunged, baring wicked, yellowed teeth. But the men gradually forced it into a narrow chute with high plank walls. A stocky, weather-beaten man with short black hair was crouched on a narrow ledge that ran along the top of the chute. He flung a leather saddle that lacked the usual saddle horn across the Appaloosa's back.

On any other occasion, Justin would have stopped to watch. But he was too worried to have any interest in the bronco or its rider. He scanned the corral area. A wiry, redheaded man led a big, black stallion from a long, barnlike structure. Justin gestured toward the redhead. "Maybe *he* knows where Sky Teacher is!"

Justin and Jenny started across the corral, but they had taken only a few steps when the black stallion reared, jerking the lead rein from the handler's grasp. It lunged forward with an enraged scream, and the man grabbed for the rein.

"What d'ya think you're doing here!" he shouted angrily. He jerked his head toward a sign that read: Authorized Personnel Only. "Can't you kids read? Or are you trying to get yourselves killed!"

They backed away. "We didn't know we weren't supposed to be here," Justin apologized. "We're just trying to find Sky Teacher. Could you tell us where he is?"

The redhead now had a firm grasp on the nervously prancing stallion, but he shook his head sharply. "I don't have time for this. You two get out of here—now!"

Justin turned away in disappointment. But Jenny took a step forward. "We're really sorry we scared your horse. But we've *got* to find Sky Teacher! It . . . it's a matter of life and death!"

The man hesitated. He glanced down into her pleading face, then looked away. "Okay, okay!" he growled. "Sky Teacher's in the arena right now doing some of that fancy riding. Then he's on for bronc riding—Black Lightning here, in fact. You two come back after the bronc riding and maybe you'll catch him."

"Thanks a million!" Throwing her brother a triumphant glance, Jenny started back toward the gate.

How do girls do that? Justin rolled his eyes and followed his sister.

They stopped to rinse their hands and faces in the cool water from an outdoor faucet, and then made their way toward the rodeo arena. It was a long, oval corral with bleachers running down both sides. At the far end was a raised stand for the rodeo judges and announcer. The bleachers were packed, and Justin and Jenny climbed clear to the top row before they found an unoccupied space. They sat down and watched the party of mounted Indian warriors who circled the arena at a full gallop. They waved their spears and let out bloodcurdling war whoops.

Justin had just picked out Dark Cloud when the war party wheeled as one and charged down the length of the arena. Then they disappeared through a high gate followed by the roar of cheers and applause. The loudspeakers blared, "And now, ladies and gentlemen, the event you've all been waiting for! Risking life and limb in chute number one, last year's state champion, Mike Black Bull on Killer Boy!"

A wide gate swung open at the far end of the arena. The white-and-brown Appaloosa lunged out, bucking and jumping sideways as it tried to rid itself of the unwanted burden. Its rider raked the Appaloosa with steel spurs, and the maddened animal reared and corkscrewed, then came down in a series of stiff-legged jumps. But the rider stayed on, his right hand gripping the reins, left hand raised high.

The whistling, stomping crowd, the hot smells of dust and horses, the vicious battle between man and animal swept Justin into the excitement around him. He shouted and stomped his feet. The ten-second horn blared, and a mounted man galloped alongside the still wildly bucking horse. The bronco rider reached over to grab the pickup man's shoulder. Swinging himself over the rump of the other horse, he slid to the ground to wild cheers and chants of "Black Bull! Black Bull!"

Justin was still caught up in the noise of the crowd when Jenny suddenly gripped his arm hard. "Justin!" she hissed. "Look who's here!"

Justin came down to earth with a thump. Philip Dumont and Yellow Dog stood directly below them. They scanned the bleachers as though looking for a vacant seat, then climbed up toward the top row. Justin glanced at Jenny with dismay as the two men found seats just a few feet away.

Seating himself with exaggerated care, Yellow Dog turned to meet the twin's hostile eyes. He stared at them for a long moment, then stretched his thick lips into a broad smile. It wasn't a pleasant smile, and Justin couldn't repress a shiver as Yellow Dog deliberately turned his back to them.

The loudspeaker was announcing the next rider—a young cowboy visiting Rocky Creek for the rodeo. But for Justin, the magic was gone. Jenny echoed his feelings as she whispered angrily, "What are *those* guys doing here?"

Justin shook his head. The young cowboy lasted only six seconds before a side jump left him loose in the saddle. The next jump tossed him over the head of the tall, raw-boned roan. There was a collective groan from the crowd. The young rider rolled over slowly as the pickup man galloped between the angry roan and the fallen rider. When he didn't get up, four men with a stretcher ran into the arena.

There was a long pause as the stretcher crew carried the young rider out of the arena. Justin glanced at Philip Dumont and Yellow Dog out of the corner of his eye. *They're sure looking pleased with themselves!* he thought worriedly. *I wish Sky Teacher would hurry up and ride!*

The crackle of the loudspeaker broke into his thoughts. "Coming out of chute number three—John McCloud on Black Lightning!"

Justin let out his breath in relief. As soon as this ride was over, they'd find Sky Teacher and tell him everything they'd discovered. Then *he* could take care of Philip Dumont and Mr. Siedman! He settled back to watch the ride. "McCloud has quite a ride waiting!" the announcer bellowed. "Let's not forget, folks—this is the horse that trampled and killed a rider at last year's championships in Great Falls!"

A killer bronco! Great! Justin watched anxiously as the wide gate marked "3" swung open. The big, black stallion left the chute in a lunge that carried it halfway across the arena. Sky Teacher had changed his chieftain's outfit for jeans and cowboy boots. He rode easily as the stallion arched its back, ducking its head between stiff-spread legs. Then the big horse left the ground, bucking viciously, and cheers of "McCloud!" and "Sky Teacher!" rose from the bleachers. There were a few boos as well, and Justin noticed a NARC emblem around the neck of one heckler in the next row.

A movement to his right drew Justin's attention from the bucking bronco. Yellow Dog and Philip Dumont both leaned forward, their eyes intent on the battle below. Both were smiling—cruel, gloating smiles! Justin drew in his breath sharply as a horrible realization gripped him.

"Sky Teacher! Watch out!" He sprang to his feet, shouting at the top of his lungs. But it was too late! The big black stallion reared, its front hooves flailing the air. It rose up and up until Justin thought it would topple backward on its rider. Then it came down hard, its back arched high.

A yellow dust cloud hung over the center of the arena, but Justin was sure he saw the hornless rodeo saddle shift as the bronco's feet struck the ground. He heard Jenny's gasp of horror and a sudden hush fell over the entire arena. Then the crowd groaned in dismay as the saddle slipped sideways and Sky Teacher was thrown across the maddened bronco's neck!

Chapter Twelve

MYSTERY SOLVED

Half lying across the horse's neck, Sky Teacher kicked the stirrups free just as another sideways lunge sent the saddle crashing to the ground. As the stallion reared and corkscrewed to the right, he slid back onto the bronco's back.

Sky Teacher rode bareback now, keeping his seat in spite of a series of vicious bucks. The crowd roared its approval. Justin and Jenny were on their feet, screaming along with the crowd as the pickup man edged close to the maddened animal. Then it was all over. Sliding over the back of the other horse, Sky Teacher dropped on his feet to the dusty floor of the arena.

The crowd—even the heckling activists—gave him a standing ovation, whistling and chanting, "Sky Teacher! Sky Teacher!" Justin and Jenny sank into their seats, weak-kneed with relief. It was only then that Justin noticed the two men slip down through the standing crowd.

"Look! They're getting away!" he said urgently. "We'd better find Sky Teacher. That redhead said we could come back after he rode."

They threaded their way as fast as they could through the cheering crowd. By the time they reached the bottom of the bleachers, Philip Dumont and Yellow Dog were out of sight. The twins hurried around the outside of the arena, then pushed open the gate that led to the corrals. The black bull was gone, but Justin caught a glimpse of its massive hindquarters moving majestically toward the chutes.

"Hey! You there!" An irritated shout brought them to a halt. A stocky Indian in his late teens moved to block their passage. His black eyes narrowed as he recognized them. "What are you two doing here?"

"Hi, Bear Paw!" Justin said. "We're looking for Sky Teacher."

"Well, you're not coming in here!" Bear Paw said angrily. "Can't you read the signs? All we need is some stupid kid spooking the broncs. You two get on out there with the rest of the tourists!"

"But we've *got* to find Sky Teacher!" Jenny insisted. "He's in trouble!"

"Trouble," Bear Paw scoffed. "Sky Teacher stirs up his own trouble. What does he expect, bringing his 'white man' religion and his 'white man' friends to the reservation!"

Justin flushed red at the young Indian's contemptuous tone. He turned on his heel. "Come on, Jenny. He's not going to help us!"

But Jenny wasn't going anywhere! Hands on her hips, she glared up at the Indian cowboy. "How can you talk like that?" she demanded. "Sky Teacher was your friend—at least until that Dumont started making everyone mad! And what did we ever do to you? Why do you hate us so much?"

Bear Paw was taken aback by Jenny's response. He fell silent for a moment, then said slowly, "I never said I hated you. You just don't belong here! And Sky Teacher—well, he's not so bad, but he doesn't belong here, either. Philip Dumont says he's destroying our culture with his 'white man' ideas. He's going to bring the anger of the spirits down on the whole reservation if he doesn't stop!"

"Philip Dumont!" Jenny's brown eyes flashed gold sparks. "How can you believe his lies? He's the one doing all that stuff to hurt Sky Teacher—not any spirits!"

"Watch it, Jenny!" Justin warned in a low voice, but she was too upset to listen.

"And that burial cave of his," she rushed on. "*He* put all that stuff there himself! We saw him, didn't we, Just—" She clapped her hand over her mouth, her eyes wide with distress as she realized what she'd let slip. Bear Paw's fists balled at his sides.

"You lie!" He was so angry that his words hissed between his teeth. "Philip Dumont has told the truth about Death Canyon. I saw the vision myself! The spirits are calling to us to protect their sacred ground."

A shrill whistle cut off whatever else he was about to say. The wiry redhead strode toward them and jerked his head toward a long, open shed with a galvanized metal roof. "Sky Teacher's over there in the barn. Come on, I'll show you the way."

Bear Paw's black eyes sparkled angrily, but he moved out of the way. They followed the man across the corral. Justin could feel the young Indian's smoldering gaze on the back of his neck. He was relieved to duck into the horse barn and see Sky Teacher standing near a wide sliding door at the far end.

A cement walkway ran down the center of the barn between two rows of stalls. Several of the stalls were occupied, and as they hurried after the redhead, a familiar dark head thrust itself over the bars and snorted down their necks. They paused to give Dark Cloud a pat.

"I probably shouldn't have gotten so mad!" Jenny said in a low voice. "It's just—well, he was a friend of Sky Teacher! I mean, Sky Teacher said he was a pretty nice guy. It makes me so furious to see him swallowing all those lies!"

"Hey, don't worry about it," Justin comforted. "It bothers me, too."

When the twins reached the far end of the barn, Sky Teacher and the redhead were bent over a saddle tossed onto the cement floor. Two other men stood watching them. One was Windy Boy the tribal chairman. The other—a tall, blonde cowboy—slapped a pair of leather straps against his hand. "Check your gear next time, Sky Teacher!" he said, shaking his head. "These are worn right through. No wonder they broke!"

"That saddle had two good straps this morning," Sky Teacher replied quietly. He gave Justin and Jenny a brief nod as they all studied the saddle.

"It sure did!" The redhead crouched down to give the saddle a closer look. "I checked all the bronco gear myself earlier today."

He took the leather straps from the other cowboy. "These aren't the straps that were on here earlier. Someone must have changed them. And look here! They didn't just break—they were cut partly through."

He gave Sky Teacher a strange look. "You got any enemies, McCloud?"

Sky Teacher didn't answer, but he looked grim. The two cowboys lifted the saddle and carried it back down the walkway.

Sky Teacher turned to Windy Boy, "Robert, you said the tribal council is signing that contract tonight. Couldn't you put it off another week?"

The elderly tribal chairman shook his head regretfully. "You know I can't do that, Sky Teacher. Dumont is leaving town, and the tribal council doesn't want to risk losing this sale."

Windy Boy lifted off his feathered headdress and scratched his head. "You said yourself it was a fair contract, Sky Teacher! Why do you continue to object?"

"It is a standard contract," Sky Teacher admitted. "But as I told the tribal council, it should include a provision for the land to be given back to the tribe if this historical reserve doesn't work out."

"We're doing what we feel is right for the tribe!" Windy Boy said sharply. "The tribe needs that money, and you have given us only unfounded accusations. Sky Teacher, you are jeopardizing any future you have on this reservation!"

"Just give me twelve hours," Sky Teacher urged. "Please trust me that far, Robert. If I don't have anything for you by morning, I'll drop any opposition to the sale."

Windy Boy folded his arms, his dark face impassive. Justin shifted impatiently from one foot to the other. If they could just get Sky Teacher alone so they could warn him! At last Windy Boy gave a curt nod. "Twelve hours, then, Sky Teacher. For the love I had for you as a boy. The others will be angry, but I will postpone the signing of the contract until morning."

The elderly tribal leader moved with quiet dignity toward the rodeo corrals. Justin turned eagerly to Sky Teacher. "Sky Teacher, we . . ." But he was already on his way to Dark Cloud's stall. He quickly led out the big quarter horse and vaulted onto his bare back. Sky Teacher looked gravely down at Justin and Jenny. "Will you two be okay on your own for a couple of hours? Some urgent business has come up."

They nodded. Sky Teacher managed a rueful smile, but the preoccupation in his dark eyes showed he was already miles away. "I'd take you along, but right now I think you're better off well away from me!"

He wheeled the big quarter horse around. Justin took a step forward. "Sky Teacher, there's—" But Sky Teacher had already kneed Dark Cloud into a trot toward the open door. "Sorry about this, kids!" he called over his shoulder. "Go on up to the house if you get bored. It's unlocked."

Justin and Jenny ran after him, waving their arms and calling. But their voices were lost in the noise of the roaring crowd inside the arena. The quarter horse broke into a gallop across the fair grounds. They dropped to a walk.

"We never even got to warn him!" Justin's face was glum.

Jenny hunched her shoulders. "Maybe we're worrying too much. You heard what he said in there! Maybe he already knows what Mr. Dumont and Mr. Siedman are up to. He probably knows he's in danger!"

"Yeah . . . well, I guess we can't do anything until he gets back anyway," Justin grumbled. "We might as well go watch the rest of the rodeo."

The bronc riding had ended by the time they got inside the arena. The half-Blackfoot, half-Sioux state champion, Mike Black Bull, was being cheered as the winner of that day's round. They watched the bull-dogging and calf-roping that followed, but Justin's attention kept wandering. He noticed Bear Paw just a few rows over. The Indian cowboy turned his head to give Justin a long, measuring stare. Justin glanced hastily away.

He looked around for Philip Dumont and Yellow Dog, but didn't see either of them again that afternoon. He *did* notice a fair scattering of NARC medallions in the crowd. Whatever Philip Dumont and Yellow Dog were up to, their followers didn't seem to be involved.

The evening powwow, a prolonged session of traditional Indian dancing and singing, was the high point of the tribal celebration. The costumes of the dancers were more fantastic than anything the twins had yet seen, with headdresses that swept to the ground and outfits heavily trimmed in furs, beads, and feathers.

"How can that guy even stand up?" Jenny pointed out a towering headpiece made from a whole buffalo head complete with horns.

The wild frenzy of the drums crept into Justin's feet. *Maybe my own great-great-grandfather stomped and pounded his spear like this before sweeping out to fight an enemy tribe.* Then he remembered with some regret that the Indian war parties were already a thing of the past by the time his great-great-grandfather came to this reservation. He glanced restlessly toward the entrance. *Where is Sky Teacher? He's been gone for hours!*

Jenny got tired of the dancing, and sat down to examine the package of Montana Indian life postcards she'd bought earlier that afternoon. She'd never seen holographic laser images on postcards before. Justin joined her and picked up a postcard and tilted it to see a 3-D image of a bald eagle flying across the Rocky Mountains.

"Yellow Dog and Mr. Dumont were the ones who cut those

straps, weren't they?" she said in a low voice. "Remember their faces when Sky Teacher almost fell?"

Justin nodded. "Yeah, it was them all right! That's what they were planning in the tepee."

"Well, remember what they said? If that didn't work, they were going to leave him 'to the spirit of Chief Thunderbird!'"

"Hey, stop worrying about Chief Thunderbird," Justin said impatiently. "Mr. Dumont just made up all that 'spirit' stuff to scare people away from Death Canyon."

"So what about White Tail?" Jenny argued. "Okay, I know the ghost didn't kill him, but something did! And what *did* we see out there?"

For the third time, something nagged at the back of Justin's mind. "I don't know! But it wasn't a ghost!"

Jenny looked doubtful, then pulled out another postcard. Justin leaned back against a wooden post. The events of the last few days—the ghost of Chief Thunderbird, the mysterious death of White Tail, the equally mysterious explosion in the church, the strange behavior of Philip Dumont and Yellow Dog— churned over and over in his mind. What was the mystery that lay behind the legend of Death Canyon?

Shifting his long legs, he thrust his hands into his pockets. His fingers touched a folded piece of paper. He pulled it out. It was the sheet of paper they'd tried to return to Mr. Siedman. Until now it hadn't occurred to him to wonder about what might be in that man's briefcase. He unfolded the paper. Maybe this would hold a clue!

The sheet of paper was part of a computer printout. The name Universal Corporation printed in the top right-hand corner meant nothing—until he remembered seeing that name on the directory of businesses listed on the outside of the office building where they'd seen Mr. Siedman and Philip Dumont.

The paper contained lists of figures and a few scattered words. He studied the computer printout more closely, puzzling over the abbreviations *n.g.* and *prod.* and the words *shale strata* and *porous rock.* The figures and words looked oddly familiar.

Justin's mind flipped back to his occasional visits to the Seattle-based offices of Uncle Pete's company, Triton Oil. His eyes opened wide with sudden excitement. *Prod.* for production. *N.g.* for natural gas. And *shale strata* and *porous rock* were terms his uncle used when he was exploring for natural gas. This sheet was part of a production estimate for a natural gas well!

"Hey, Justin, who does this remind you of?" Jenny thrust in front of him a postcard of an Indian chieftain mounted on a small pony.

Absently, Justin tilted the card from one side to the other, watching the stern, dark face disappear and reappear as he changed the angle of the holographic image. Then he stiffened. Stunned, he looked from the postcard to the sheet of computer paper. One by one, the missing pieces clicked into place. He knew he was right! This had to be it!

"Well? Doesn't it look like Chief Thunderbird?" Jenny reached for the postcard, but she dropped her hand when she saw the expression on his face. "What's the matter?"

He gave her a blank look. "I've got it!"

"Got *what?*" Jenny demanded.

"Everything! The ghost—the explosion—Death Canyon! I know how they did it—and more importantly, I know why!"

Chapter Thirteen

THE WARNING

Justin sprang to his feet as an awful thought struck him. "Jenny, you were right! Death Canyon *is* dangerous! We've got to tell Sky Teacher!"

"Justin, what are you talking about? *What* did you find out?"

But Justin was already on his way out of the dance enclosure. Grumbling, Jenny picked up the postcard he had dropped and followed him. Justin waited only until he saw Jenny coming. "Hurry up, Jenny! We've *got* to find Sky Teacher right away. I just hope we're not too late!"

He took off down the road that led from the fairgrounds into Rocky Creek, running faster than he had ever run before. For once, Jenny could hardly keep up with him. He didn't slow down until he heard an engine roaring up behind them. Dodging to the side of the road, he glanced back to see a battered green pickup racing toward them.

Dropping to a walk, Justin waved the pickup on by. But instead of passing, the truck slowed down. Bear Paw leaned out the driver's window. "You kids need a ride home?"

"No, thanks!" Justin answered shortly. "We're just fine!"

But the pickup idled along beside them. The young Indian

cowboy jerked his head toward the passenger side. "Get in! I want to talk to you."

Justin scowled. He didn't trust anyone who was a friend of Philip Dumont. But his chest burned from running, and he knew they didn't have much time! Jenny didn't hesitate. She hurried around to the passenger door. "You can run the rest of the way if you want, Justin. *I'm* going to ride."

Justin reluctantly climbed in after her. Bear Paw stepped on the accelerator. "I heard someone tampered with Sky Teacher's saddle this afternoon," he said abruptly as the pickup moved off down the road.

"That's right!" Justin nodded. "Someone cut the straps so they'd break on him!"

"That's bad! I saw a guy get killed once when his saddle broke. But if someone cut those straps . . . that means . . ." Then he took a deep breath as though he couldn't believe his own thoughts. "Philip Dumont told us it was the spirits who brought destruction down on the church last night. But it takes a man to cut a strap! Who'd want to kill Sky Teacher?"

"We *told* you!" Jenny burst out. "Mr. Dumont and Yellow Dog cut those straps—just like they blew up the church and killed White Tail!"

"Yeah?" Bear Paw demanded sarcastically "So how come *you* two know so much about it?"

"Because we—" She broke off at Justin's warning nudge.

Bear Paw scowled. "I figured you two would find a way to blame Philip Dumont! Everyone knows how Sky Teacher's been fighting him. But just tell me this! If Philip Dumont is such a bad guy, why would he give the reservation a million dollars?"

"That's easy," Justin said quietly. "He wants that land!"

Bear Paw threw him a startled glance.

"Philip Dumont is a crook," Justin went on. "We can't tell you how we know, but he's been fooling you all along! He's fooled the whole reservation."

"I don't believe you," Bear Paw said flatly, but for the first time he sounded uncertain, and his dark eyes were troubled. "Philip Dumont is the best thing that ever happened to this reservation. He's given us back our hope, our pride in who we are! There's no way he'd do something like that!"

He gave a quick nod then continued. "No, Philip Dumont was right! It was the spirits that brought destruction on Sky Teacher. As for those straps—that was probably one of those off-reservation NARC activists. They don't like him at all!"

Justin shrugged. "You'll find out for yourself soon enough!"

Bear Paw didn't answer. He drove in silence the rest of the way.

Justin stared out the window. Maybe he was wrong. *No—this is the only answer that fits!*

Justin leaped out of the pickup even before it stopped. To his relief, Sky Teacher's pickup was in its usual spot. Jenny thanked Bear Paw as Justin bounded up the front steps.

"Sky Teacher!" he called. No answer. His eyes fell on a sheet of note paper lying on the kitchen table. He quickly read it, then slammed out the back door and headed for the stable.

"What's wrong?" demanded Jenny.

He waved the note at her. "It's too late! He's already left."

"Where'd he go?" Jenny snatched the note. "Sky Teacher," she read aloud. "The land sale is a fraud. We must talk. Meet me in

Death Canyon." The note was signed in careful printing by A.T. Siedman. Jenny glanced at her watch. "It's almost eight o'clock. He probably went out there hours ago!"

"Sky Teacher doesn't know that Siedman's behind all this!" exclaimed Justin. "He won't know it's a trap! They just want to get him out to Death Canyon!"

He pounded his fist against the wooden railing of the stall. "Mom and Dad should be back by now! *They'd* know what to do!"

"They'll be in tonight," Jenny reassured him.

"But that'll be too late!" Justin cradled his throbbing fist in his other hand. "They'll leave him in Death Canyon and blame it on Chief Thunderbird. We've got to do something!"

The Appaloosa whinnied questioningly over the top of its stall, and Justin gave it an absent-minded pat as he thought. He turned to give the mare a long hard look, then opened the stall and led her out.

"Come on, Jenny!" he urged, lifting the saddle from the wall. "We don't know how long ago he left. Maybe we can still get there in time!"

"In time for what?" Jenny planted her foot. "I'm not moving one inch until you tell me what's going on!"

"Not now. I'll tell you on the way," Justin slipped the bit into the horse's mouth. "You get the rest of the straps." Pulling a pencil stub from his pocket, he scribbled on the back of the notepaper: We're going to Death Canyon. Sky Teacher is in danger. Justin & Jenny

Hanging the note on a nearby nail, he helped Jenny tighten the last strap. She scrambled into the saddle behind him, still determined to get some answers. But there was no chance to talk as Justin kicked the Appaloosa into a trot across the road. The mare seemed to sense his urgency and broke into a distance-eating gallop as soon as they reached the open prairie. The first star hung low above the horizon by the time they rounded the back of the mesa and left the grasslands behind. Justin saw that the trail into Death Canyon was now clearly marked by scattered piles of horse dung. When he urged the Appaloosa down the ravine, Jenny tapped his shoulder.

"You're not just going to ride in there! I thought this was supposed to be a trap!" She gestured toward a rock outcropping just a few yards away. "That's where we went in last time. Maybe we should climb up and see if anyone's around first!"

Justin gave a reluctant nod and turned the Appaloosa down into the other gully. He held the mare to an ambling walk and strained his ears for sounds of other riders. But he only heard the throb of distant Indian drums. When the gully ended, they left the Appaloosa with its reins trailing and scrambled up the rock face. Dropping to their bellies, they inched forward to the edge of the limestone wall. To Justin's disappointment, the plateau below them stretched empty and quiet to the darkening shadows that marked the canyon edge.

"Oh, no! They must have already come and gone!" Swinging himself over the edge of the steep wall, Justin felt for a foothold. Half sliding, half jumping down to the plateau, he broke into a run toward the edge of Death Canyon. A terrible fear gripped his heart. *What if we're already too late!*

When Jenny caught up with him, he was already down on his stomach, peering down into the canyon. The darkening twilight cast a long shadow across the basin floor, but he could still make out the vulture lying where it had fallen beside the bloated body of the dead deer. Stretched nearby was a doglike animal that Justin guessed to be a coyote, tempted into the canyon by the promise of fresh meat. But there was no sign of what Justin most feared.

"He's not here!" Justin let out a breath. He felt a little foolish at the thought of their frantic ride. "I guess he never came. Dumont and Yellow Dog must have gotten tired of waiting and gone home."

"What *are* you talking about?" Jenny stayed well away from the edge as she peered cautiously into the canyon depths. She had never liked heights, and this drop-off was steep enough to make her dizzy. "What killed those animals down there? What *is* this big secret you found out about Death Canyon? Justin, I've waited long enough! If you don't tell me what's going on here, I'm going to do something—something awful!"

"You mean, you haven't figured it out? It's pretty simple, really!" Jenny took a menacing step toward him, and he added hastily, "It's natural gas, of course!" When Jenny looked blank, he repeated, "Don't you get it? There's *natural gas* down there! That's what Mr. Siedman and Mr. Dumont were after all this time."

"How do you know that?"

"You know how I'm always reading Uncle Pete's magazines and stuff for his oil consulting work?"

"Yeah, I don't know what's so interesting about all that stuff—"

"Well, the gas collects in porous rock like that limestone or sandstone down there. It gets sealed under layers of nonporous rock far below the earth's surface. And it'll just sit there until someone like Uncle Pete comes along and figures a way to get it out."

Jenny nodded. "And I suppose that has a lot to do with why this is called Death Canyon?"

"Right, sometimes an earthquake or a crack in the limestone rock will let gas escape to the surface." Justin pointed out a black shadow behind the piled-up boulders on the basin floor. "If you breathe enough, it will kill you—like those animals there! That's probably what started the legend." He frowned. "The only thing is—I think natural gas is lighter than air. So it should just float up—unless you're in a closed building or something, you'd have to have an *awful* lot of gas to kill all those animals. And that much gas . . ."

". . . is worth millions!" Jenny finished. "No wonder Philip Dumont wants Death Canyon!" Edging a little closer to the rim to study the dead animals and scattered bone piles at the bottom of the canyon, she added with somewhat grudging admiration, "It makes sense, all right! But I sure don't see how you figured it all out."

Justin pulled the sheet of computer paper from his pocket. "This gave me the idea. Mr. Siedman said he'd found no trace of natural gas or oil on this land, but these are production estimates for a natural gas well. And look at those initials!"

"D.C.!" Jenny picked out the initials that were scattered through the list of figures. "Of course! That must stand for Death Canyon!"

Justin nodded, his green eyes gleaming with excitement. "That's when it all started to fall together—White Tail, that explosion last night, the way it was so hard to breathe, and that awful headache! Remember last year in Glacier Park when we accidentally left the camp stove in Grandpa Hollow's camper running all night? We all had headaches in the morning. Grandpa said we'd all have suffocated if the windows hadn't been open!"

"You mean, *you* left it running!" Jenny retorted. "Anyway, that stuff smelled awful! It stunk up the whole camper!"

"That's what fooled me—*and* the police chief!" Justin admitted. "I'd forgotten that natural gas *has* no smell. They put that awful smell in when they process it so people will know when they've got a gas leak. Otherwise, people could suffocate without ever knowing."

"Then those animals—and White Tail!" Jenny turned pale as she eyed the dead animals below. "So that's what Mr. Dumont meant when they said they'd 'leave Sky Teacher to Chief Thunderbird!' But what about the ghost? We weren't the only ones to see him!"

"I have an idea about that!" Justin scrambled to his feet to study the limestone wall that ran around the plateau.

"You've *always* got an idea," Jenny muttered. But she followed willingly as Justin trotted back to the spot where they had climbed down. He eyed the dozens of shadowed openings that pockmarked the rock face. "It's got to be around here somewhere!"

He poked his head into a shallow opening a few feet to his right. "We've got to check anything that looks like a cave!"

Jenny moved left along the cliff face. Justin was climbing out of the empty hole when he heard her stifled shriek. "Jenny, are you okay?"

"I'm fine!" Jenny answered crossly. She stooped again to peer into a wide opening a dozen yards along the wall. "It was just that 'sacred burial cave' of theirs! What am I looking for, anyway?"

"I'm not sure—some kind of machine!" Justin hurried toward another opening halfway up the wall.

The last of twilight was fading into night when Justin heard the low whistle they used as a signal. He hurried back along the rock wall until he spied Jenny swinging her legs over the edge of a narrow ledge just above his head. Climbing up beside her, he gave a whistle of appreciation. The sophisticated piece of equipment inside the small cave behind her looked like something out of a science fiction movie. Squeezing through the narrow opening, he began pushing the buttons at random.

"What is it? Some kind of camera?" Jenny poked her head into the cave, then spun around with a jerk. A strange glow was lighting up the night sky. A shimmering, half-solid figure appeared at the head of Death Canyon.

"Chief Thunderbird!" she exclaimed as the silent horseman galloped down the canyon.

"It's just a holograph—a 3-D image!" Justin was pleased with his surprise. "I once read an article about holograph projectors. They use them for special effects in movies."

"Hmmph!" Jenny grunted as the ghostly figure disappeared around the cliff wall. "It sure fooled me! I've never even *heard* of a holograph projector—and I'll bet no one around here has either!"

"I might have thought of it earlier if I hadn't been so scared!" Justin admitted. "I didn't even think of that article until you showed me that postcard of Chief Thunderbird!"

Jenny wrinkled her nose with disgust. "So when Mr. Siedman

and Mr. Dumont found out about the natural gas, they must have decided to use Chief Thunderbird and the legend of Death Canyon to steal this land from the tribe. What a bunch of total jerks!"

"I'd say that's a pretty good summary of the facts, Jenny." The familiarity of the voice made them both spin around.

"Sky Teacher!" squealed Jenny half sliding, half falling from the ledge. "You're okay! Where have you been?"

"I got back home half an hour ago and found your note announcing you two were off to rescue me from terrible danger! And to think I left you behind because I thought you'd be safer away from me. You had me worried sick!"

"We found a note from Mr. Siedman and thought Philip Dumont and Yellow Dog had you!" explained Justin defensively. "Wait until you hear what we heard today."

Sky Teacher perched on a pile of boulders and listened patiently to their tumbled words. Soon all the pieces seemed to fit. The moon was over the cliffs now, casting a pale light across the plateau. Sky Teacher nodded approval when they finished. "That ghost was the last puzzle piece I hadn't put together. Good work, kids!"

"Then you already knew about the natural gas?" Justin asked with some disappointment.

"Well, I suspected there was something valuable out here from the lengths to which Philip Dumont was willing to go. But it was your Uncle Pete who suggested that natural gas best fit the facts."

"Uncle Pete?" Justin and Jenny couldn't hide their surprise.

"That's right! Your uncle has been running some inquiries for me. As you know, he's got a lot of friends in high places. When I left the fairgrounds, I rode cross-country to a rancher friend who owns the closest fax machine. It's taken until now to get some plans worked out. I think the tribal council will find the information Pete faxed me very interesting!"

Sky Teacher rose to his feet. "We'd better get you kids back to the reservation. Your parents should be home pretty soon."

He jerked a thumb toward the canyon as the ghostly figure of Chief Thunderbird—which seemed to be on some sort of automatic replay—began another sweep across the sky. "Maybe you'd better turn that off before we go. I'd rather not attract any more attention!"

"I'll do it!" Jenny said quickly. "I push the red button—right, Justin?"

A cloud shut out the moonlight, and Jenny seemed to disappear into the night, but Justin could make out a dark form ducking into the narrow mouth of the cave. He turned back to the tall shadow that was Sky Teacher. "I guess the tribal council won't sign that contract now!"

"They sure won't!" Sky Teacher agreed. "Not once they've heard what's really going on out here."

"And now, the tribe will have money from the natural gas. And I'll bet they'll kick Philip Dumont and his bunch off the reservation." Justin paused for a breath, then added thoughtfully, "I wonder what they'll say when they find out all that stuff about Chief Thunderbird and Death Canyon was a lie."

"What a pity you'll never get a chance to tell them," a smooth voice announced from the blackness behind them.

Chapter Fourteen

DEADLY SLUMBER

The cloud thinned over the face of the moon allowing enough light for Justin to see the man striding toward them, two shadowy forms close behind. The powerful flashlight swept across Sky Teacher's dark features. Then the light locked onto Justin's face, and he shielded his eyes with his arm.

"Great!" Philip Dumont snarled. "What's the kid doing here?"

The beam leaped upward and across the overhead ledge and the black mouth of the small cave. The light glinted off a glass lens. "Been snooping again, Sky Teacher?"

Justin didn't dare glance up toward the ledge, but he edged away from the rock wall. "Yeah! We saw your machine, all right!" he said loudly. "And we know how you're cheating the reservation, too!"

The powerful beam swung back to follow him just as he hoped it would. Anything to keep them off of Jenny's trail. The moon emerged from behind the cloud and shed a silver radiance on the other two men. Yellow Dog, like Philip Dumont, still wore ceremonial Indian dress. But Mr. Siedman looked as out-of-place as ever in his neat business suit. Justin swallowed hard as he caught the unmistakable shape of the handguns Philip Dumont and Yellow Dog carried.

"I knew you'd be stupid enough to fall for that note, Sky Teacher!" Yellow Dog sneered. "I've been following you all afternoon—clear out to that ranch and back—just waiting for you to start out here!"

"Sky Teacher didn't—" Justin burst out angrily, but Sky Teacher's warning hand on his shoulder silenced him.

"Yellow Dog," he spoke quietly, ignoring the big man's boasting, "*you've* got quite a record—everything from armed robbery to assault and battery."

Yellow Dog looked startled. "Who told you that?"

"You've been working for Mr. Dumont here ever since he came out West more than a year ago." As he talked, Sky Teacher walked out from the black shadow of the rock wall into the silver moonlight of the plateau. Philip Dumont and Yellow Dog had to swing around to keep their guns trained on him. Yellow Dog waved his gun menacingly. "Stand still or I'll shoot!"

Sky Teacher stopped obediently. The other three men now stood with their backs to the cliff. Sky Teacher *had* understood what he was doing. Yellow Dog shoved Justin over beside Sky Teacher.

"And Philip Dumont! Or shall I call you 'Paul Dillon'? A con man with several arrests for fraud under different names. Strangely enough, I couldn't find you listed on the rolls of any Indian tribe in North America. You sure had a lot of people fooled!"

"I thought I made a pretty good medicine man!" Philip Dumont mocked. "It was rather amusing to see how much of that nonsense about 'sacred lands' and 'ancestral spirits' your people would swallow."

Justin kept a wary eye on the rock wall behind their captors. But he gave no sign when he saw a sudden movement at the mouth of the cave where the holograph projector was hidden. Instead, he looked at the three men. Yellow Dog had turned sideways, his gun still aimed at Sky Teacher.

"Yeah, just like that explosion you rigged last night!" Justin spoke loudly to cover any noise that Jenny might make. *She's got to get away and get help!*

"You thought you were so cool making everyone think it was the spirits! All you really did was shut the windows and pump the church full of natural gas. Talk about stupid! You could have killed Jenny and me!"

His distraction seemed to work. Yellow Dog turned and growled, "If it were me, I'd have left you there. But Dumont's chickenhearted NARC pals didn't want anyone to get hurt."

"It wasn't difficult to get a few tanks of unscented natural gas around here," Philip Dumont admitted smugly. Justin let his breath out slowly as the shadowy figure disappeared over the top of the rock wall. *Good thing she's the one with the quiet feet!* The brief flicker of Sky Teacher's eyes told Justin that he too had seen, but he continued the conversation.

"They never did manage to convict you, Dumont, did they? Somehow you've always managed to come up with *very* good lawyers! Lawyers supplied by Universal Corporation—the same company who donated the funds to set up your Indian Historical Foundation. Universal Corporation is your real employer, isn't it? And I don't suppose it's any coincidence that it also happens to be the same company that tried to buy this land a year ago!"

He spun around to face Mr. Siedman, who stood to one side

with his hands in his pockets, listening with quiet interest. "A company which, when traced back through all those dummy corporations and trusts, turns out to be owned by you!"

Mr. Siedman showed no surprise. "I see you've done your homework."

"I sure did, Siedman! I also uncovered the fact that Universal Corporation has been involved in several suspicious land deals in the past few years—land that always turned out to be extremely valuable! You moved out here just over a year ago from your New York office, posing as a geologist—which was your original career. I assume you had already discovered the significance of the legend of Death Canyon."

"I've made several major finds around the world by taking native superstitions seriously," Mr. Siedman answered amiably. "A casual conversation with a client from this area brought the legend to my attention. I investigated and—well, you know the rest."

"We had that contract sewed up," Philip Dumont interjected, "until a bunch of politicians sold it off to the reservation right under our noses!"

Sky Teacher frowned. "What puzzles me is how a gas leak of that magnitude has escaped notice all these years. It's been decades since anyone brought up that legend of Death Canyon as a place of bad luck."

"An earthquake sealed off the old leak a hundred years ago," Mr. Siedman answered indifferently. "It was actually an accident that revived the legend."

"That's right," Philip Dumont interrupted again. "We were doing a little drilling down there—just to see if it was worth our money. We lost a worker before we realized we'd hit the jackpot! One of the men—a Navajo from New Mexico—quit on us right away. He insisted that the spirits had killed his friend. When we lost the contract, it seemed convenient to revive the old legend—and add a few modern touches."

"Hey, boss!" Yellow Dog demanded. "Are we gonna stand here jabbering all night? Dumont and me—we've got to get back to the party!"

"No, I think we've heard enough." Mr. Siedman turned to Sky Teacher. "You're an intelligent man, McCloud! I'm sure you realize we can't let you—or the boy—get back to the tribe. I have too much time and money invested in this deal."

He nodded to the other two men. "You know I don't like to be involved in these little affairs of yours! I'll be heading back to town. Just let me know when our problem is resolved. Without McCloud, I doubt we'll be bothered by any further inquiries for a while."

"You know someone's going to uncover Mr. Dumont's fraud here sooner or later!" Sky Teacher raised his voice as Mr. Siedman started to walk away.

Mr. Siedman stopped and turned around. "Mr. McCloud, I'm getting the impression that you are trying to delay my departure!"

Sky Teacher ignored his remark. "But that's what you intended all along, isn't it? A few months from now, Philip Dumont's 'sacred burial ground' and the spirit of Chief Thunderbird will be 'discovered' to be fakes. Dumont will get the blame, of course! But by that time he will have disappeared—and reappeared elsewhere under a different name.

"After a few months, the disillusioned Foundation will sell off the land—not back to the tribe, but to the Universal Corporation. By the time the discovery of natural gas is announced, it will be too late for the tribe to do anything about it. Have I missed anything, Mr. Siedman?"

"No, I think you've just about covered it! And now, Mr. McCloud, I really must be going." Mr. Siedman glanced down at Justin. "I really *am* sorry it had to end this way."

Justin stared at Mr. Siedman in horror as the meaning of his words sank in. Mr. Siedman seemed like such a quiet, ordinary man. But he was really the worst of the lot! He wouldn't do any actual violence himself, but he'd sure close his eyes while someone else did!

People don't really matter to him, Justin thought savagely. *Just money!*

Mr. Siedman disappeared into the shadows. Philip Dumont waved his gun toward the canyon rim that cast a black shadow across the far end of the plateau. "Get walking!" he ordered.

Sky Teacher didn't move. He glanced from one man to the other, his gaze watchful and measuring. "Why should we—when you're going to kill us anyway?"

Yellow Dog grabbed Justin and yanked him back against his powerful body. Grinding his gun into Justin's ear, he sneered, "That's easy! Either you walk—or I blow the kid's head off right now!"

Justin was so scared he could hardly breathe! The gun was cold and painful against his ear, but he didn't dare flinch. He sensed Sky Teacher's muscles tense, then relax as Sky Teacher recognized the hopelessness of trying to intervene. Philip

Dumont thrust his gun into the small of Sky Teacher's back. "Enough of this! Get moving!"

Yellow Dog tightened a steel arm around Justin's chest. "Same to you, kid! Any funny business from you, and we'll take care of your friend here before Chief Thunderbird ever gets a chance!"

Justin felt sick as Yellow Dog pushed him across the moonlit plateau. *He* was the one who had led them into this trap! Sky Teacher would be perfectly safe right now if Justin hadn't galloped madly out here to rescue him. Sky Teacher reached out a hand to steady him as he stumbled blindly over an outcropping of rock.

"This isn't your fault," he said, as though reading Justin's thoughts. *"They're* the ones responsible for this. Not you."

They had reached the canyon edge now. Sky Teacher turned to the two armed men. "You can still walk away from this, you know. You two have at least avoided murder until now."

"Oh, there won't be any question of murder!" Philip Dumont pulled out a handful of what looked like the terry cloth sweatbands Justin had often seen on joggers. "Just two more deaths chalked up to the legend of Death Canyon."

He handed his gun to Yellow Dog, who shifted to keep both prisoners covered. Yanking Sky Teacher's arms behind his back, he twisted one of the terry-cloth bands tightly around his hands. "These here are a little invention of my own. They don't leave marks the way a rope does."

"At least let the boy go!" Sky Teacher urged, as Philip Dumont pushed the missionary to the ground and repeated the operation on his ankles.

"And have him run straight to the cops?" Yellow Dog sneered, jabbing Sky Teacher in the side with his foot. "No way! This deal will set us up for life! Besides, the boss gets pretty ugly when he's crossed."

Philip Dumont had produced a coil of rope from somewhere. Cutting off a length, he pulled Sky Teacher's feet up behind him. Twisting the rope around the terry-cloth bindings, he lashed them to his bound wrists while Yellow Dog did the same to Justin, leaving both of their captives lying helplessly on their sides at the canyon edge.

"Tomorrow Yellow Dog here will 'remember' having seen you two ride off toward Death Canyon," Philip Dumont said cheerfully, slapping a piece of masking tape across Justin's mouth. "When you two are discovered, I'll give my final performance. The theme—how Sky Teacher's stubborn worship of the 'white man's God' brought the wrath of the spirits on him. Too bad you two won't be there to hear it!"

He moved over to slap several layers of tape across Sky Teacher's mouth. "You know, my family has always considered themselves Christian—not that we've ever been to church! It's kind of ironic that—between your death and my preaching— the two of us are going to put an end to all that Bible stuff on the reservation!"

Sky Teacher just looked at him gravely. Philip Dumont turned away with an unpleasant chuckle. "Come on, Yellow Dog! Let's get this over with!"

Using the long coil of rope to form a harness around Sky Teacher's bound form, the two men lowered him over the canyon edge as though he were a sack of wheat. Justin eyed the guns they had dropped on the ground nearby, but he couldn't move an inch to reach them.

Yellow Dog scrambled down the cliff face and came up a moment later with the rope. Twisting it around Justin, they pushed him over the edge. Justin tried to control his panic as they lowered him into the dark chasm. Then a sudden slip of the rope left him spinning helplessly against the rock wall of the canyon.

"Careful!" he heard Philip Dumont snap. "We don't want any marks on him!"

Justin landed roughly on the ledge where the skeleton had been found some fifty feet below the edge of the canyon. Lifting his scraped face, he saw Sky Teacher lying unmoving further down the ledge.

Philip Dumont lowered himself down the canyon wall. Rolling Justin onto his side, he pulled away the rope harness. "We want this to look natural. But we can't untie you until you're unconscious. That might take awhile this far up."

He spoke as though commenting on some ordinary event. Shining his flashlight down the slope that ended in the boulder-filled hollow another thirty feet below the ledge, he added, "We're okay right here for a few minutes. But we don't dare go down there without gas masks. I'm afraid this'll just have to do. It might take a little longer, but don't worry—they say it's just like falling asleep!"

Cupping his hands around his mouth, he called up to the top of the cliff, "Hey, Yellow Dog, go turn that projector on!"

Turning his flashlight on Justin's face, Philip Dumont gave another unpleasant chuckle. "We'll let any watching Indians have a last vision of 'Chief Thunderbird' riding over Death Canyon to claim his final victims."

Justin glared furiously over the tape that bound his mouth. "Are you afraid, boy?" Philip Dumont mocked. "I thought you'd be in a hurry to see that heaven you Christians are always talking about!"

Justin was shaking with anger as Dumont climbed back up the cliff. Sure he was afraid! But he also knew that Philip Dumont was right. If he died, he would soon be in heaven with his Savior Jesus Christ. But what about Sky Teacher's hopes and plans for the reservation people? What about all those tribal members who would be fooled into believing that angry spirits had killed Sky Teacher and Justin?

Justin twisted and tugged desperately, but Philip Dumont had been right. The terry cloth bindings didn't cut into his skin, but neither did they budge! Justin finally gave up when he almost rolled off the ledge. *God, why are You letting this happen?* he screamed in his head. His eyes focused on a dark figure silhouetted against the canyon rim far above. *Don't You care if they follow Philip Dumont? Don't You care if they believe in You?*

His head was beginning to spin, and he knew he was feeling the effects of the invisible gas wafting up from the deadly hollow below. With fresh panic, he fought against his bonds, but it was useless. Was Sky Teacher having any better luck? If so, Justin couldn't hear him, and he was far too close to the edge to dare shift around to where he could see down the narrow ledge. *Is Sky Teacher already unconscious?*

Exhausted, he lay still, panting. His eyes traveled up to the star-spattered night that stretched far above the canyon. *Are you still there, God?*

His eyes were drooping again, but somehow it didn't seem so

important anymore. He'd done everything he could, and all he wanted now was to close his eyes and go to sleep. Yellow Dog must have reached the holograph projector because the image of Chief Thunderbird was shimmering above the rock face at the end of the canyon. *You think you've won! But you haven't— not while Jenny's still out there and free! She'll make sure you get what's coming to you!*

Through a mist, he watched the ghostly horseman gallop across the sky overhead. As his eyes drooped shut, he mumbled against the masking tape. *Jenny, don't let them get away with this!*

Chapter Fifteen

THE NARROW LEDGE

"Wake up, Justin! Oh, please wake up!" The frantic whisper penetrated the blackness. "Oh, no! It *can't* be too late!"

"Let's get him up."

A searing pain ripped across his face and brought him back to a semiconsciousness. A hard hand slapped him on both cheeks. Sleepily he forced his eyes open. Sky Teacher was bent over him. Justin winced as he touched his stinging mouth. Then he realized that his bonds were cut and the tape ripped from his mouth. Shaking his head groggily, he struggled to his feet. He blinked at the dark silhouette of his sister on the ledge in front of him. "Jenny, what—"

"Shh!" Justin followed Sky Teacher's quick glance upward to where two dark forms stood outlined against the starlit sky. He could hear Sky Teacher's labored breathing, but the big Indian missionary seemed otherwise alert. Justin's head was still spinning, and he sank back down onto the ledge.

"Come on! We've got to hurry!" Jenny tugged frantically at his arm. "Justin, you've got to get out of this! The air's better up higher!"

Justin couldn't think straight, but he obediently followed his sister up the side of the canyon, fumbling for footholds in the sheer rock face. Sky Teacher steadied his wobbling legs from behind. They had climbed only a few feet when he fell forward onto a narrow path that crawled upward across the rock wall.

Justin's vision went black as he struggled to pull himself to his feet. He swayed dizzily. But as Jenny tugged him up the path—actually little more than a ledge just wide enough for their feet—a breeze stirred through the canyon and brushed across his hot face. He gulped eagerly at the fresh air. His head began to clear, and he climbed more quickly.

Death Canyon was vaguely trough-shaped, narrow at the canyon floor and gradually widening toward the top. The canyon was only a few hundred yards long, and at the top end it rose in a perpendicular rock face to meet a dry creek bed whose torrents swept through the gorge during the spring rains. The path led upward across the canyon wall toward the creek bed. Within a few minutes, they had climbed beyond the reach of the poisonous gas pumping into the hollow below the ledge.

Breathing more easily as the widening canyon walls allowed the natural gas to disperse into the air, Justin wondered that the two figures standing on the canyon rim hadn't spied their escaped captives. Then he realized that while the full moon was reflecting softly from the canyon floor and the plateau above, the canyon wall up which they crept was in the blackest shadow. They were invisible to anything but a direct searchlight. They covered more than half the distance along the ledge when a light blinked on, probing the depths where he and Sky Teacher had just been.

"Hey, they're gone!"

"What do you mean they're gone! They can't be!" Curses and

shouts floated down into the canyon. Justin quickened his footsteps as the powerful searchlight began to sweep across the rock walls. But it was no longer possible to move quickly. They were now far above the canyon floor, and the path under their feet had narrowed to a ledge barely wide enough for their feet. Backs to the wall, they crept sideways along the cliff face.

"There they are!" A shout rang out across the canyon. With horror, Justin realized that their ledge was now curving around to meet the creek bed, and the ghostly radiance of the moon now shone brightly on their precarious perch.

"Justin . . . Jenny, we'd better get out of here fast!" Sky Teacher said in a low voice, as two dark figures raced toward them along the canyon rim.

They were now only a man's height from the top of the cliff. From here, they could easily scramble to the plateau. But the limestone wall that circled the plateau ran right to the edge of Death Canyon. Their only choices were to cut back across the plateau in full view of the two running men or to climb the remaining distance across the canyon wall and up that dry creek bed.

"Come on, Jenny!" Justin urged impatiently. "Let's get moving!"

But Jenny was no longer moving. She stood pressed against the cliff, her fingers glued to the rock behind her. Glancing beyond her, Justin saw why she had frozen. The narrow ledge broke off right at her feet. Only a dozen yards separated them from the creek bed that spelled escape. There were ample hand and footholds in the limestone rock. But directly below them the canyon wall sloped in a steep incline that ended at the canyon floor some eighty feet down.

Justin knew how much his twin hated heights. Eyeing the difficult climb across the face of the precipice, he asked in amazement, "Did you come across there earlier?"

"I guess so!" Jenny answered weakly. "I just knew I had to reach you!"

"Kids, we don't have much time!" Sky Teacher reminded. Following his urgent glance, Justin saw that Philip Dumont and Yellow Dog were getting closer.

"Here, I'll go first!" he told Jenny. "Sky Teacher and I will help you across."

Justin edged around his sister, careful not to look down. Turning to face the rock wall, he felt for a foothold. When he had found a secure place for both feet, he held out his hand to Jenny. Firmly grasping her other hand, Sky Teacher helped Jenny inch her way over to Justin.

Justin moved as quickly as he dared from one foothold to the next, but they had covered only half the distance between the narrow ledge and the shelter of the creek bed when a sudden shower of dirt rained down on them. Justin craned his neck to look up the few feet that still separated them from the canyon rim.

"Thought you'd get away!" Yellow Dog growled. He kicked another shower of pebbles and dirt over the edge.

Sky Teacher steadied Jenny against the cliff face. "Hang in there," he whispered.

Yellow Dog's face widened in an evil grin as he leveled his handgun. Justin froze as he heard the distinct click of the hammer being cocked.

"Don't be a fool!" Philip Dumont knocked Yellow Dog's gun upward. "It's got to be an accident! Besides, there are easier ways!"

Tucking his own gun into his belt, Philip Dumont picked up one of the small boulders that littered the plateau floor. Stepping to the canyon rim, he said coldly, "Sky Teacher, I really *am* getting tired of you!"

The three figures clinging desperately to the side of the cliff could not even duck. But just as Philip Dumont raised the heavy stone above his head, the roar of an aircraft broke the night stillness, followed by flashing lights that swept down to hover only yards above the plateau.

The stone crashed to the ground. Philip Dumont and Yellow Dog threw their arms over their faces as the helicopter sent a blast of wind and dirt into their faces. Then an amplified voice ordered, "This is the police! Throw down your weapons and put your hands over your heads!"

Justin felt like shouting his thankfulness. Instead he scrambled up to the canyon rim and pulled himself onto the plateau. He peered up cautiously, still not convinced that danger was past. But Yellow Dog and Dumont stood hands raised high as they stared with baffled rage at the police helicopter that was just settling onto the plateau.

Satisfied that the police had things under control, Justin leaned down to haul up Jenny. But he had just grabbed her hand when Philip Dumont whirled around, his right hand reaching toward his belt. "You haven't won this yet, Sky Teacher!" he screamed out, his voice twisted with hatred.

As Justin yanked Jenny up to the plateau, he saw with horror the ugly shape in the angry man's hand. Instinctively, he stepped in front of Sky Teacher, who already had his hands on the canyon rim. But Philip Dumont wasn't even looking at Sky Teacher.

Striding to the edge of the canyon he aimed his gun at the moonlit boulders on the canyon floor. It took Justin a long second to realize what he had in mind.

"No, don't shoot!" he shouted, lunging for the gun hand.

But it was too late! Philip Dumont pulled the trigger. Justin held his breath. If the bullet could only bury itself in the limestone walls without striking a spark on those granite boulders!

But Philip Dumont hadn't missed! A sheet of blue fire exploded through the canyon, streaming into every hollow and crack in the limestone walls as the vast pool of natural gas ignited. Clapping their hands to their ears, Justin and Jenny fell to the ground as the earth shook and rumbled beneath them. Then, seemingly in slow motion, the entire canyon wall broke away and tumbled into the black depths below.

Justin and Jenny scrambled to their feet as the thunder of the rock slide died away. With horror, they stared into the shattered chasm. The basin floor of Death Canyon lay buried under gigantic chunks of limestone. There was no sign of Sky Teacher!

Chapter Sixteen

CANYON BLAST

"Oh, Sky Teacher!" Jenny whispered hopelessly. "No!"

Justin stared down into the canyon, blue flames still licking the walls. The police helicopter had landed somehow, its spotlight flashing rhythmically across the plateau. But Justin couldn't take his eyes off the tumbled remnants of the cliff wall. He hardly even noticed the running figures that yanked Yellow Dog and Philip Dumont to their feet or the footsteps that joined him on the shattered rim of the canyon. It just couldn't be true! After all they'd gone through—after their own miraculous escape—he couldn't believe that Sky Teacher was really gone!

Then another revolution of the powerful searchlight flashed across the canyon. Justin blinked in mingled shock and hope. Was that a dark shadow rising to its feet on a newly-formed ledge partway down the cliff face?

Jenny's hand slid into Justin's. "It can't be—is it Sky Teacher?" she said uncertainly.

Then a somewhat winded voice called up calmly, "Ron—Pete, if you'd throw down that rope, I'd sure appreciate a lift out of here!"

"What?" They whirled around. For the first time, Justin

realized who it was that stood beside them on the canyon rim. "Mom? Dad?" His voice broke in an incredulous squeak as he spotted the big man with the look of a youthful Santa Claus standing just beyond his parents. "Uncle Pete? Is that *you?*"

"Let's save the greetings until we get John out of there," Uncle Pete said calmly. Stepping to the canyon rim, he yelled down, "Hey, are you okay down there, McCloud?"

"I'm fine," Sky Teacher's firm voice floated up.

Uncle Pete grabbed the coil of rope. "You want to give me a hand, Ron? We'd better get John up."

Dad and Justin both helped Uncle Pete let out a long line of rope.

"Can you climb, John?" called Dad. "We can come down for you."

"I can climb. Just hurry—there's still enough gas down here to make my head swim!"

It didn't take them long to haul Sky Teacher over the canyon rim. Other than a slight limp and a long scrape down his face, he seemed unhurt. Justin and Jenny both stared at him with unbelieving eyes, but it was Justin who spoke.

"I thought you were . . . I mean, when the cliff fell . . ." He peered gingerly over the edge.

Sky Teacher brushed at the tattered remnants of his shirt and jeans. "To tell you the truth, I can hardly believe it myself! I felt myself going when the explosion knocked me loose. But somehow I managed to grab onto something—a piece of rock, I guess—and slide down to that ledge."

He swung around to look down at the massive blocks of limestone piled up across the canyon floor. "Only God's protecting hand could have brought me out of that," he said soberly. "I *felt* the chunks of rock falling all around me, but not one flying piece actually hit me."

Pulling out a handkerchief, he dabbed at the graze. "I'm afraid I've got plenty of bruises and scrapes to show for it, though!" He turned to Uncle Pete. "It's good to see you, Pete! I was beginning to think you weren't going to make it."

Both Justin and Jenny's mouths fell open. There was amusement in Sky Teacher's deep voice as he explained, "I told you kids that Pete was investigating Mr. Siedman and his bunch for me. But I didn't get a chance to tell you he was so concerned by the results of the investigation that he decided to fly out here himself—though I hadn't expected him to arrive quite so conveniently." His explanation was cut off as a police lieutenant hurried toward them.

"Well, folks," he asked briskly, "is everyone okay here?" He ran an expert glance over everyone, then went on without waiting for an answer, "I'm going to need you all at the station to get your statements. But I'd like to get these two out of the way first."

He jerked his head toward Philip Dumont and Yellow Dog, who were standing sullenly near the helicopter, their arms handcuffed behind them. "They're a dangerous pair, so I'd rather not have any of you in the chopper when we take them in—for your own safety! I've called for a backup chopper. Would you mind waiting here until it arrives?"

"We'll be fine!" Uncle Pete assured him. "You just go on."

"I don't get it!" Justin burst out as the police lieutenant walked away. "Where did all those policemen come from?" He eyed his parents and Uncle Pete with bewilderment. "And you guys! How did you all get out here, anyway?"

"Yeah—and just in time to save us!" Dropping to the ground, Jenny folded her arms across her knees. "Look, if we've got to wait for that helicopter, you guys might as well tell us what's been going on—before we die of curiosity!"

Everyone laughed as they settled down on the ground to wait. Sky Teacher admitted, "I must say I'm a little curious myself! I didn't realize any of you—or the state police—knew the way to Death Canyon."

Uncle Pete's full, red beard split in a smile. "There's no mystery about it, John. After I talked to you, I took the first flight available to Great Falls. Helen and Ron had just gotten in when I called from the airport. They'd found the kids' note—and Mr. Siedman's—and were extremely worried. It sounded like something pretty serious was going on, so I called a contact of mine with the state police in Great Falls. . . ."

Justin and Jenny flashed a grin at each other. Was there anywhere in the world where Uncle Pete *didn't* have a contact?

"With the information my investigation had turned up, it wasn't hard to convince the state police to fly out to the reservation. We swung by the parsonage to pick up Helen and Ron—hoping, of course, that you three might have returned by then. But as to how we got out to Death Canyon—" Uncle Pete stopped to glance around. "Where *is* that kid?"

The helicopter was taking off now, the whine of its engine rising to a scream. It lifted into the air. Justin's eyes sharpened in sudden disbelief. A lone figure had separated from the blowing dust on the plateau floor. "Bear Paw? What's *he* doing here?"

"Oh, there he is!" Uncle Pete raised his voice over the roar of the departing helicopter. "Come on over, Bear Paw."

Bear Paw trudged toward the group on the canyon rim, his back bent against the backwash of the helicopter. He stopped a few feet away as though not sure of his welcome. "They kicked me off the chopper," he said sullenly.

"We were wondering when you were going to join us, Bear Paw!" Mom welcomed the Indian cowboy into the group with a gentle smile. She turned to Justin and Jenny. "Bear Paw saved your lives, kids! If he hadn't shown us the way to Death Canyon, we'd never have made it in time."

They both stared at Bear Paw with incredulous eyes. "But he's on *their* side!" Jenny said indignantly. "Why would he help *us?*"

"Yeah!" Justin looked straight across at the young Indian. "I figured you'd run right to Mr. Dumont after you dropped us off this afternoon!"

"Well, maybe I did!" George Bear Paw's dark face was defiant as he dropped to the ground. "I mean, I figured Dumont should know what you guys were saying. Only—well, I couldn't find him or Yellow Dog anywhere—and they'd told us all to be there for the powwow. Dumont said he was going to make some special speech. It seemed kind of strange that he wasn't there!"

Bear Paw glanced sideways at Sky Teacher. "So I figured— well, if one of our guys *did* tamper with Sky Teacher's saddle, it wouldn't hurt to talk to him, just to see what he had to say!" A sudden bewilderment replaced the defiance on his face. "Only . . . only when I got there, these police were all over the place, and they were saying things—anyway I said I'd take them to Death Canyon just to show them Philip Dumont wouldn't do anything like . . . that!"

Bear Paw's dark features twisted. He turned his face away, his shoulders hunched. Justin couldn't help feeling sorry for him. He was seeing the Indian cowboy in a different light—not a tough, rebellious NARC activist, but a boy not too many years older than himself who was hurting at the loss of a hero he'd counted on and respected.

"Well, thanks for saving us, anyway!" he said gruffly. "I really thought we were gone down there!"

"It was God who brought you to see me tonight, George," Sky Teacher said gently. "He used you to save our lives."

Bear Paw didn't answer, but his shoulders relaxed, and he turned slowly to face the rest of the group. They could now hear the throb of an approaching aircraft. Sky Teacher, leaning back to watch the flashing red-and-blue lights sweep down over the plateau, said quietly, "You know, it may sound strange, but in all that happened, I never doubted that we'd be rescued.

"You see, I knew Philip Dumont was right. If I died— apparently at the hands of the 'spirits'—it *would* mean an effective end to the preaching of the gospel here on the reservation. With the church building gone, it's unlikely the tribal council would allow the Indian Bible Mission to send another missionary. I couldn't believe that God would allow His work here to be destroyed. Of course, I never expected Bear Paw or . . ." Sky Teacher reached out to ruffle Jenny's dark curls with one big hand, ". . . or Jenny here. In fact, if it hadn't been for her, you all would have *still* arrived too late!"

"Hey, yeah!" Justin demanded. "How *did* you do it, anyway? We thought you'd gone for help!"

Jenny shrugged, looking embarrassed and pleased at the same time. "After what you said about White Tail and that gas, I was afraid there wouldn't be time to get help. So I crawled along the top of the cliff and came down in the shadows. I couldn't hear what they were saying, but when they started pushing you over the edge, I knew I had to do something. I climbed down into that creek bed and—well, you know the rest."

She shuddered. "By the time I got down there, I thought I was too late."

"Hey, we all made it, didn't we?" Justin gave her a comforting squeeze. "Thanks for coming back for us! You're a real hero—I mean heroine!" He broke off with a sudden thought. "Hey, we forgot the horses! They're still out there!"

"Don't worry about the horses," Sky Teacher said. "We'll send someone to pick them up." He laughed as Justin let out a yawn that almost split his face. "I think we'd better get you kids to bed!"

But it was the early hours of the morning by the time the police helicopter finally dropped the Parkers and Sky Teacher off at the parsonage. As though ashamed of his earlier admissions, Bear Paw maintained a moody silence all the way to Great Falls. The scream of the engines made conversation almost impossible anyway. At police headquarters, an officer led George off to make his statement. Justin didn't see him again that evening, and when he questioned the police clerk, he was told that the Indian cowboy had left the station.

They were just reboarding the helicopter when the police lieutenant strolled up. "I thought you'd like to know that Dumont and Yellow Dog are both cooperating with the police. They're in such a hurry to throw the blame on each other that they've spilled out all they know about Mr. Siedman and his land fraud. And you'll be glad to hear we've got Mr. Siedman in custody as well. He was clearing out of his office with a briefcase of money and incriminating papers when we picked him up."

It was noon on Saturday by the time Justin and Jenny rolled out of bed. They took their parents down to the fairgrounds, but the color and noise of Indian Days now seemed a little tame after the excitement of the previous night. A swarm of reporters had invaded the reservation, and the only topics of conversation were the bombshell of Philip Dumont's fraud and the exciting discovery of natural gas. Justin saw the blonde reporter one last time posed in front of a group of whirling Indian dancers.

"In a bizarre twist to this reservation saga," she said to the news cameras, "new evidence has shown Dumont's famed 'sacred burial ground' to be the final resting place of a U.S. Cavalry soldier. What he was doing in Death Canyon we may never know. But one thing's for sure! The discovery of natural gas here is the dawn of a new era for the Big Sky Indian Reservation!"

Uncle Pete and Sky Teacher spent the day in meetings with the tribal council. Later, they joined the Parkers on the front porch where an evening breeze was cooling the air. Sky Teacher filled them in on the details.

"The tribal council feels pretty angry and foolish about Philip Dumont's deception. But, of course, they're excited about the natural gas. They've voted unanimously to give the development contract to Triton Oil. Pete and I will make sure the tribe gets a fair deal."

"That's just great . . ." Dad stopped in mid-sentence as a pickup full of laughing Cree adults and children stopped in front of the parsonage. A slender young woman of medium height with long, blue-black hair and an olive complexion climbed out. She waved good-bye as the pickup drove off, then walked quickly down the path to the front porch. Stopping at the bottom of the wooden steps, she looked up and said softly, "Hello, John."

Justin had never seen Sky Teacher speechless before. He rose to his feet with wide eyes. Before he could get a word out, the young woman ran up the steps and threw her arms around his neck and kissed him. She pulled away, and turned to face the row of interested faces.

"Hi there!" she said, her dark eyes twinkling. "You must be the Parkers. John's told me so much about you!"

At last, Sky Teacher found his voice. "In case you haven't guessed, this is Marie!" He kept an arm around her shoulders, but asked with some bewilderment, "What are you doing here? I thought you were in California!"

"I saw you on the early news today. Oh, John, you could have been killed! Naturally, I caught the first flight out. That nice family was at the airport picking up a friend for Indian Days and offered me a ride." Her chin tilted with determination, she added, "John, I know you haven't wanted me mixed up in all the trouble out here. But if God has brought us together, then He wants us to help each other in the hard times as well as the good."

She turned an engaging smile on the Parkers. "Don't you agree?"

The Parkers were all grinning widely. Leaning over to Justin, Jenny whispered loudly, "I have a feeling there's going to be a wedding." The red stain on Sky Teacher's bronzed cheekbones told them that he'd overheard, but he didn't seem to disagree.

The next morning, Sunday school was held in front of the charred remnants of the old church building. There were no interruptions this time. Most of the NARC activists, resentful at finding they'd been tricked and used by Philip Dumont, had already left the reservation. But the circle was large today—many who had stayed away the last few months looked sheepish as they sat down. Sky Teacher opened his Bible just as Windy Boy walked up and sat beside the Parkers. After Sky Teacher closed in prayer, he walked over to greet the elderly tribal chairman.

"I have long worshiped the spirits of my ancestors," said Windy Boy. "But I have watched you. Your God protected you against great evil. Today the words from your God's book were good ones. I will come to hear them again."

After lunch, Justin and Jenny began reluctantly loading their belongings into the SUV. Dad was due back at work in two days, and it was a long drive back to Seattle. Uncle Pete would stay long enough to organize the exploration crews, and Marie would fly home that afternoon to give notice at her job and pack her things. Jenny's prediction of a wedding had turned out to be an accurate one.

"I wish we could stay for the wedding," Jenny complained.

"We'll expect you next summer," Sky Teacher assured her, eyes twinkling. "With a little less excitement, hopefully."

He gave Justin a handshake and Jenny a big hug. "I'm deeply grateful to you, Justin—Jenny! Without your help, Philip Dumont might have gotten away with his scheme, and I might have been driven off the reservation—or worse! Now there's a real chance for my people."

Marie added a hug of her own. Justin and Jenny were climbing into the back seat of the SUV when they saw Bear Paw striding across the grass. *There's something different about him*, Justin thought. Then he realized that the Indian cowboy no longer wore his NARC medallion—or his usual sullen expression.

He hardly glanced at the Parkers or Marie as he strode up to Sky Teacher. "I . . . talked to Philip Dumont, Sky Teacher!" he blurted out. "I just couldn't believe—I thought there was some mistake! But he laughed at me—said I was a fool." He looked down at his feet.

"I guess I *am* a fool! But he made it sound so good—all that stuff about being proud of ourselves—of a great future for our people. He gave us hope. But it was all a lie!"

"There *is* hope for us . . . for the future," Sky Teacher answered quietly. "But it is Jesus Christ who gives us that hope."

Bear Paw lifted his head. "I . . . I had been thinking about following your God before Philip Dumont came to the reservation. Do you think—I mean, is it too late?"

Sky Teacher grinned, "Of course not! Why don't you come on up to the house, and we can talk about it."

Justin gave Jenny the thumbs-up as the SUV pulled out onto the dusty road. Craning their necks, the twins watched out the back window until the little wood-frame parsonage and the three people walking toward it disappeared from around a bend in the road. Then they let out a simultaneous sigh. Dad threw them a sharp glance.

"Well, it's back to work for me and school for you two!" he said cheerfully over his shoulder. "Think you're ready to handle your new school?"

The Parkers' neighborhood had been rezoned that summer.

Instead of returning to a nearby middle school, the twins would start the school year next week at a large junior high some distance from home.

"Sure!" Justin replied. "Other kids got transferred too. I'm sure we'll find some kids we know. But school sounds pretty tame after the last few days. Unless we stumble onto another mystery." He looked over at Jenny. "You know, we do seem to have a knack—"

"No, thanks!" Jenny leaned back and folded her arms behind her head. "I don't plan to get involved in any more mysteries. Besides, nothing exciting ever happens at school."

"Yeah, I guess you're right!" Justin agreed glumly. Little did they know how wrong they would be!